The
RESISTANCE
WIFE

BOOKS BY GOSIA NEALON

Gosia Nealon

The
RESISTANCE
WIFE

bookouture

Published by Bookouture in 2023

An imprint of Storyfire Ltd.
Carmelite House
50 Victoria Embankment
London EC4Y 0DZ

www.bookouture.com

ISBN: 978-1-83790-895-0
eBook ISBN: 978-1-83888-823-7

To my beloved sister Kasia – the strongest woman I've ever known.
I love you and miss you so much.

PROLOGUE

ANNA

15 March 1934, Germany

With my face buried into à Persian rug, now spoiled by blood and tears, I try to suppress my pain. This time he was even more brutal than before.

I don't know how long I've been lying down like this, unable to move. It isn't the physical strength I'm lacking—it's more my mind that's slipping into darkness. What would it be like to stay there forever, free from Helmut?

Our wedding a year ago was a glamorous affair, attended by the most powerful dignitaries in Berlin. They did it out of respect for my father, a famous engineer highly recognized by the newly appointed chancellor, Adolf Hitler.

I will never forget that day and how excited I was about my gorgeous wedding dress, but most of all, I looked forward to beginning a new chapter with my charming and handsome fiancé. Life was going to be a fairy tale.

Initially, I thought that Helmut's reserve came from his shyness, but the night after our wedding proved me a fool. There was no caressing or kissing. He was rough and brisk, and then he rushed out of the room leaving me alone for the night, humiliated and hurt. Now I'm not that naïve anymore.

This has been my life since then. Plus, occasional beatings when he doesn't like the way I look at him, or the tone of my voice. Today, he lost his temper after finding out that I auditioned for a play in a local theater.

"Anna, darling, are you there?" My mother's quiet voice and insistent knock at the door jar me from my reverie. What is Mutti doing here? But then I remember that we have plans to go out shopping in the afternoon.

Pain surges through my body as I move upward. I would hate for Mutti to see me in this condition.

But the door swings open, and she charges in, saying, "Wilhelm told me that Helmut left a while ago, so—" She freezes, gaping at me. Then she leaps forward, and without another word, she helps me get up and settle on the bed. She wraps my face between her hands. Her gentle touch feels comforting, but her eyes reflect guilt. "I'm so sorry, darling. I'm so sorry," she whispers in a broken voice.

I clear my throat, unable to hold back tears. "It's not your fault." I snuggle my head into her chest and sob.

She holds me so close for a long moment. I really meant when I said it wasn't her fault. I understand her weakness when it comes to my father and forgave her a long time ago. Still, sometimes I can't help but feel betrayed.

At the very beginning of my marriage, I confessed to my parents about Helmut's mistreatment. I'll never forget that dreadful moment in my father's library. My mother sat motionless with tears in her eyes, but Papa wasn't touched by any of my words. He coldly reminded me that there had never been a divorce in the history of his respected family, and he would not allow one now that he was a prominent member of the Nazi Party. He hinted that there must be reason for Helmut's hostility toward me and that I had to try to be a better wife, and most of all, not to provoke him.

I sensed I could not count on my mother's support, so I left my childhood home with a broken heart, swearing to never again look at my father or say another word to him. And I have kept my promise.

"I want you to know that I don't agree with your papa, making you feel like all this is your fault. He is so very wrong about that." She sighs and runs her gentle fingers back and forth through my hair. "His family traditions and the need to be respectable in the eyes of German society cloud his common sense. You know he works day and night just to please the chancellor and the Nazi Party with his genius projects. Like it or not, it's what brings purpose to his life."

Of course, Mutti is right. My father takes his role in Hitler's party very seriously. He is obsessed with the chancellor's views on how to improve Germany. To be honest, I never had interest in politics and Mutti always made sure we never spoke of it at home. But when my father one day gifted me a book written by Adolf Hitler, I felt obliged to read it. I expected *Mein Kampf* to be a positive outlook on how to approach new changes and cultivate a strong country. Instead, I couldn't believe how awful and hateful it was. The man is a lunatic and I truly hope his position in our government will lessen. At the same time, it's so hard to comprehend that my intelligent papa shares his views.

"That man is deranged, Mutti, and I don't understand why Papa is so smitten with him."

She glances around and says, "I agree with you but there is nothing we can do, and now we need to take care of you. Since your father fails to protect you from this monster, there is only one thing we can do."

I lift my head to meet her now determined gaze. When she's like that, the blue of her eyes become even lighter. These are rare moments, as my father dominates every aspect of her being, of her will. Still, the love between them is unconditional. My father never raises his hand to her, and always treats her with respect and tenderness. He is the ruler in the family and my mother accepts it —it is easier that way. I was raised to believe that a husband is to protect his wife, and as young and naïve as I was when I married, I expected the same from Helmut. My only ambition was to be a good wife, but in return I receive beatings and disrespect.

"Papa would rather let him kill me than allow divorce," I say and force a shaken laugh.

"I know," she says. "It's why you must run away from here to where you will have a good life. And I happen to know just the place."

I shake my head. "It's impossible. I know you mean well, Mutti, but how can I run away from here? It won't take long for Helmut to find me, and then—"

"You can do it." Her intense gaze puts me at a loss for words. It's clear she has a plan, and she is more determined than ever to set it in motion.

Sparks of hope slip into my veins. I want to believe that life holds more for me than an abusive husband and tears, with all my heart. "How?"

"I received a letter from a lawyer in Poland who informed me that I've inherited a dwelling in Warsaw."

I open my mouth, about to voice all my questions, but she touches her finger to my lips. "I know this sounds surreal but perhaps one day there will be a better time to explain it all to you. Now, my darling, we need to free you from this hell. No one knows about this, not even your father. Only a few people in Warsaw: the lawyer named Witek who contacted me and an older woman who checks on the tenement. Rest assured, that Helmut will not think to look for you over there." A wicked look covers her face. "To be safe though, you cannot use your married name. In May, your husband and Papa plan to go hunting for a week. That's when you will take a train to Warsaw. I will inform Witek ahead of time and he will help you settle in. It's your opportunity to begin a new life, sweetheart."

My head is spinning. "But I don't speak any Polish."

She smiles. "I will teach you."

I raise my brow. "You?"

She nods. "When I was little, Grandma employed a Polish housekeeper whom she insisted spoke to me in only her own language. Now I know she did it to give me the little part of my heritage."

True to her words, Mutti spends the next months teaching me Polish. She also arranges for things in Warsaw. And as the day approaches, I grow more and more in this stubborn determination to never again be vulnerable. From the moment I leave Berlin, I will be strong and independent, and I will never let anyone hurt me again.

PROLOGUE

MATEUSZ

18 June 1939, Warsaw

When I think of my family home, the first thing that comes to my mind is a sponge cake with fresh strawberries. Today is no different as the sweet aroma fills the entire house while we celebrate my little sister's eighteenth birthday.

Busy with my doctor's practice and volunteering at an orphanage, I visit my parents rarely these days. At twenty-eight I'm happy with my life. Busy but happy. After my father's retirement, I took over all his patients, but I particularly enjoy helping children.

"So, what's the plan for the rest of the evening?" I ask, pretending to not have planned anything else, while we sit at a dining table enjoying Mama's stuffed cabbage with mashed potatoes and cucumber salad.

An instant disappointment comes to Wanda's face. "Nothing. I guess I can play piano with Tata and then do some reading."

I try to hide a laugh. Teasing my little sister has always been one of my favorite things. "Since you already have plans, I will have to return these to Mietek." I take out two tickets and place them on the table. "Too bad these seats are in a first row of the amphitheater on the water in your favorite Royal Baths Park."

She jumps from her sit and envelops me in a hug. "You're the best brother ever. We should leave soon." The eagerness in her voice warms my heart. I would do anything to make my little sister happy, just like she is in this very moment.

"I don't think this is a good idea." Mama's gruff voice takes the smile from Wanda's face. "Wanda is too young to be out this late," she continues as Wanda returns to her seat.

"I'm eighteen now and can do as I please." Stubbornness never works on our mother.

Mama's fist lands on the table making me jump. "As long as you live in this house, you will obey the rules." This is why I don't visit much anymore. There is always a conflict between them. I prefer the solitude of my flat in the city center.

The air thickens by every second but Tata clears his throat and says to Wanda, "That's not the right tone, young lady. You ought to show respect to your mother no matter what." His tone is stern but also somehow gentle. "Please, apologize." Never before have I heard him raise his voice at her. He simply doesn't have to. She always listens to him.

"I'm sorry." Wanda's voice is quiet but she doesn't look into Mama's angry gaze. My sister has a lot of fire in her, fire that only my father knows how to tame.

He takes her hand in his. "Darling, I'm sure Wanda will be just fine under Mateusz's care."

"You know I'm not in good enough health for this." She gets up and gathers empty plates. "Be sure to bring her back before midnight," she says without looking at me. My mother is hurt but once more she did it to herself. She has the power to mend her relationship with Wanda but she chooses not to. Instead, she keeps building a wall because of what happened in the past.

I follow Mama to the kitchen and embrace her in a hug. It

doesn't matter how wrong I think she is; she is my mother, and I
will always cherish and appreciate her.

The Royal Baths Park in the city center is a huge complex of
palaces, monuments and gardens. But to my sister with her
artistic soul, it's more than just that. She spends her every free
moment here, claiming it restores her belief in the beauty of this
world. I don't argue or make fun of her. After all, we all need a
place of restoration like this. To me it is my work at the clinic
and the orphanage.

We walk through chestnut and spruce alleys populated
with sure-footed squirrels. In the distance, peacocks greet us
with their high-pitched cry, a strange sound I would not mistake
for any other.

Once we reach the open-air amphitheater on the east bank
of the park's south pond, we navigate through crowds of chatting people to the front row of bench seats. The statues of
ancient poets fence in the enchanted amphitheater. The stage
directly in front of us lies on a small island and only a narrow
stream separates it from us and the rest of the audience. To our
right, a stone monument of a lion guards the scene that imitates
the Roman Forum's ruins.

My sister's face shines with happiness and excitement. I try
to take on some of her euphoria and breathe in the intense scent
of wet earth from the pond. It works like aromatic oils calming
and slowing down my mind. I'm finally a part of the buzzing
excitement in the air. I take my sister's warm hand and for the
next couple of hours we live in Shakespeare's world.

The whole time I can't take my eyes off the blonde,
gorgeous actress who plays Juliet in her rosy-peach and yellow
dress. I'm taken aback by how innocent she seems. She speaks
in accented Polish. There is a beauty about her that words can't

capture. That's all I want to do: watch her while I forget to breathe.

Wanda leans toward me and whispers, "My friend Anna plays Juliet. Isn't she amazing?"

So, she is the German friend my sister keeps raving about. "She is a magnificent actress, indeed," I say, making sure to sound neutral. Better my sister doesn't know the fire this angelic-looking woman causes inside me. The teasing would never stop.

After the play ends, Wanda insists we rest on the bench near the famous Palace on the Water bound by two arcaded bridges. We watch in the pond the reflection of the palace's elegant columns and windows.

"Do you think that type of love is even possible? The one Juliet and Romeo shared?" Wanda's voice is shy but her eyes still reflect captivation. "I mean, look at Tata and Mama." She pauses as if trying to choose the right words. "I know they love each other but there is no magic between them."

My sister is still very naïve and believes that one day a charming prince will arrive to fall in love with her. Maybe it's time to help her realize the truth of this world? "That type of love brings only pain. The one our parents share is real." The moment I say it, I regret being the one taking away the enchantment of the evening that I wanted so much for her to have. "But what does a serious doctor like myself know about love..." I playfully nudge her arm with mine and smile.

The initial hint of disappointment in her eyes changes into laughter but she stays serious. "Have you ever fallen in love?"

The answer comes with ease. "Never."

"Wanda, my dear, I thought it was you." The familiar voice of Juliet causes my heart to skip a beat.

"Anna, please join us." Wanda takes her hand and pulls her between us on the bench.

Sweet, rosy fragrance tickles my nostrils. *Not only beautiful looks, but also sweet fragrances. Such an intriguing woman.* Now, when closer, she doesn't seem so innocent. Despite her youthful looks, I guess she is closer to my age. Her sad eyes betray it.

She smiles and gazes at me. "It's nice to finally meet you, Mr. Odwaga. Wanda told me so much about you."

I know it is a lie as my sister isn't a talker and she likes to keep our family affairs private. "Please, call me Mateusz. Mr. Odwaga suits my father more." I extend my hand.

She takes it, sending a weird current through my skin. "Well, then you call me Anna."

I can't comprehend why I suddenly feel so nervous. There is just something about her...

"So, what's your opinion about the war?" Wanda blurts out. She must sense the awkwardness between us.

A cynical smile covers Anna's mouth. "If you are asking me, I'm sure that Herr Hitler is way too smart to be starting one soon."

Her words free me from this state of bliss in an instant. "*Frau,*" I say, "I hope that your Führer won't prove you wrong."

PART 1

THE WAR

"True love brings pain
True love pulls at your heart
And it's never enough to touch it
Without hurting your loved one
So, kiss me, my darling, kiss me today
Let me feel your every breath..."
~Anna Otenhoff

ONE

ANNA

30 September 1940, Warsaw

"I feel so useless," I say to Witek, the lawyer who handled my mother's affairs years back. Now, he's more of a friend to me, someone I can trust unconditionally. There aren't many people in my life I can think of this way. Since the war started, he's closed his offices, afraid of being arrested by the Gestapo. They did it to most of our intelligentsia. Those people never came back from wherever they took them to. I wonder if they are still alive.

"You shouldn't feel that way. Not a beautiful and independent woman like you," Witek says and puffs on his cigarette. We sit in my flat's kitchen, on the second floor of the tenement my mother inherited. Thanks to this wonderful gift, I was able to start my life over. In fact, it was a very happy life until the war broke out.

"All these awful rules are being enforced to degrade another human being. Did you know that now the sign *Nur für Deutsche* is placed on all street cars indicating that the front sections are available only for Germans? Poles are allowed only in the back. Even more horrendous is the fact that Jews can only use public vehicles marked as *Only for Jews*. I can't stand this nonsense."

"I saw." He sighs. "I have a feeling that we're still to face much worse."

I light a cigarette and breathe the smoke in. It always gives me pleasure and a feeling of control. This, and the heavy makeup I apply to my face every morning. Both help me pretend to be sophisticated and not give a damn. At least on the outside. The inner Anna is still insecure, even after six years of freedom from Helmut.

"You're right. They won't leave anyone alone. I've already received so many offers from the director Igo Sym to play in his Theater der Stadt Warschau. I've been politely postponing my answer because I know that if I refuse him, he will send the Gestapo after me." I nervously stub out the cigarette in the ashtray and whisper, "But I will never be a part of the awful Nazi propaganda. Never." I give a shaken laugh. "As you see, my friend, my situation is rather complicated."

He creases his broad forehead. "You know I have always had great respect for your grandmother and your mother, bless their souls, so I will give you the advice I believe is right for you." He looks around as if there is a possibility someone is eavesdropping.

The way he brought up my mother was very respectful, but still a sudden wave of sadness overtakes me. It has been two years since she passed from cancer. She never mentioned her illness in her letters. She was always cheery and lovely, so I thought she was living her life to its fullest. When Witek brought the devastating news to me, my entire world crashed. I couldn't find the courage to attend the funeral and face my past.

I push back my sad thoughts and say, "I would like to hear your input."

"First, you must tell me if you would be willing to risk your life fighting Hitler." His gray eyes drill into mine as if he is trying to detect the slightest trace of betrayal or lie.

I sensed a while back that he was involved with some sort of movement against the Nazis, but I didn't expect he would be so straightforward with me. "Yes. With all my heart." I truly mean it.

He runs his hand through his thick brown hair. "I trust you, Anna. From the moment you arrived here so fragile and afraid, you were like a daughter to me, so I will be honest with you." He takes a drag from his cigarette and exhales clouds of smoke. "What I'm going to propose would give you a perfect excuse to reject Sym's offers but would also put you at terrible risk. One that can be taken only by those who are willing to sacrifice their lives for their homeland. I know you love this country with one half of your heart, but the other half belongs to Germany. So, please think about that before agreeing to what I'm about to suggest." He stubs out the cigarette in the astray and takes a sip of an ersatz coffee supplied by Wanda's mother. "By the way, as a German citizen, I find it hard to believe you have no access to real coffee?" There is no accusation in his tone, only curiosity.

"Why would I enjoy the luxury while people around me suffer? Especially as my whole heart belongs to Poland. The memory of the time spent with my mother is the only thing I cherish when it comes to Germany." I hold his gaze. "It didn't stop Chopin from giving his whole heart to this land even though he was only half-Polish." At my words, I see a flicker of emotion crossing his face. I have convinced him.

His expression grows serious. "Very well then." There's a pause. "I always wondered why you never changed the former café downstairs into living quarters?"

"I was actually hoping to, one day. Maybe after I retire from acting."

"You have so much potential that could be used toward an important cause." He leans back and grins. "What would you say to re-opening the café, to entertain German officers and dignitaries stationed in our city?"

Just the idea repulses me. Before I'm able to open my mouth to protest, he continues, "But in truth, it would be our way of fighting them."

"Our?" I ask.

"The resistance. We are here, Anna, and you can help. You would lure them here with the promise of good food and entertainment, and we would have a source of valuable information. Your last name alone is enough for them to trust you. Your father, Francis Otenhoff, holds a prominent position as one of Hitler's most valued engineers. That fact will make things easier and put you in a good stand to deal with many aspects, such as food inspectors. Trust me, your input will significantly help us to free our country but you will have to play a very dangerous game. I believe that every seed of resistance in this country will one day decide our victory, as unbelievable as that might sound."

When I realize he's waiting for my response, I clear my throat. "The whole thing does sound dangerous and brings goose bumps to my skin." At that very moment I wonder at the lightness in my chest. "But I also know it's the right path for me."

He exhales loudly but the sadness doesn't leave his eyes. Maybe he thinks this mission is doomed. "Glad to hear it. I was thinking you could name it Café Anna."

"Do you know what it was called before?"

His lips form a gentle smile. "Café Nadzieja."

"*Nadzieja...* Hope," I whisper. "No, that won't work now. Café Anna it is."

"You can always rename it after the war once your clientele changes. Let's keep hope in our hearts."

"People will think I'm a Nazi traitor," I say.

"Let them. It will give you credibility. After the war, your name will be cleared and you will be among Polish heroines."

If I didn't know Witek, I would think he was teasing me, but he isn't. I know he believes in every word he says. People like him are born to lead. In that moment, I can't help but wonder what path Helmut has taken. Did he join Hitler and his forces? Surely he did. My only hope is that he never ends up in Warsaw. That would be a disaster.

TWO

ANNA

After Witek has gone home, I can't help but think of Mutti. I take out one of her first letters in which she explained so much to me. Somehow, every time I touch it and read it, I feel closer to her.

12 July 1936

Dear Anna,

Oh, my darling, how I enjoyed your last letter. I'm so thrilled that you secured a position in Polish theater. I know your career will be successful and you will live your life to its fullest. It's what I've always wanted for you, to be happy.

There is this one thing that keeps haunting me. I promised you before you left to explain how I got to inherit the tenement. Now it's time you learn the truth even though it's not easy for me to talk about it. I'm so sorry I have to do it in a letter, but who knows when I'll see you again. For your safety, we must stay apart.

At first, I assumed that the lawyer mistook me for someone else when he contacted me about the inheritance. But in that envelope, there was another small one with my name on it. The letter I found inside explained everything to me as it was written by a woman named Róża who claimed to be my biological mother. When she was sixteen, she gave birth to me but she couldn't keep me because she was from a poor family. When her parents found out about her pregnancy, they threw her into the street. Desperate and heartbroken, she found an orphanage but she could not find the strength to give me away. She loved me.

It's how my parents, a middle-aged German couple, found her—holding me and weeping in front of the orphanage. You know how soft-hearted Grandma always was. Bless her soul. After hearing the Polish girl's story, Grandma announced that they would adopt the baby. She received some resistance from Grandpa of course, but in the end, she was able to convince him. At that time, they'd already given up hope on having their own children, so they took me as a gift from above. They traveled with me to Italy, and some time later, they went back to Germany announcing my birth. Anyway, they never told me about it. Everyone believed I was theirs because of my blonde hair and blue eyes. I wish I could ask them why they kept it from me. Maybe they thought it was better that way. You spent so much time with them before they passed away and I'm sure you remember how warm and compassionate they were. The fact that they hired a Polish housekeeper whom they asked to teach me Polish, speaks volumes. It was their way of giving me something from where I truly came. I don't hold a grudge toward them. I trust they did what they thought was the best for my future. At the same time, I can't help but wonder how different my life would have been if I'd known her while growing up.

Anyway, my biological mother found a way to flee from poverty. In her letter, she informed me that she was nearing her

*final days and that I was her only child. She never married
either. It seems to me she was an independent woman through
her adult life.*

*At the time of receiving the letter, your papa was abroad
on a business trip and wasn't due to return for a few weeks.
This is why I decided to travel to Warsaw, of course, in secret.
I told everyone I was visiting my relative in Bavaria. I got to
spend two beautiful days with her, my biological mother. She
was bedridden, but her mind was clear. Perhaps one day if you
would like, I'll tell you more about her and how she wanted to
know everything about you. One day I will get to hold you
again and I will tell you all about her. But when I do it, I want
to have you next to me, my darling daughter. I dream that day
will come soon.*

With love,

Your Mutti

I let my tears roll down my cheeks and smile. I know that
writing about it was not easy for her and that there is so much
more she wanted to tell me. I fold and kiss the letter. *You never
got a chance to tell me the rest, Mutti. How could you when we
never got to meet again?* Those sacred, maybe painful, feelings
couldn't be put on paper, they had to be told in person, so our
tears could meet. Our hearts will unite again.

THREE

MATEUSZ

29 October 1940

No one ever sees me walking the streets without a purpose. Even when I was little, I always had a plan in my head. But on this cold October day, I'm not myself. I stop at the end of Miodowa Street unable to gather my thoughts. Whatever is on my mind, is just a jumble of things I can't sort through.

After a year of German occupation, nothing in this world makes sense anymore. There are no good things awaiting us, just memories of terrifying events of the past year. They closed the schools. They packed into trucks my former professors from the university and took them to unknown places. There are rumors of the forest shootings in the village named Palmiry, done late at night. Among the lost ones was my dear professor Wieńkowski. They have captured so many people. No one believes they will ever come back. No one believes they are still alive.

After this, I reopened my doctor's practice even though my father kept convincing me that I would get arrested like the others. I took the risk because I couldn't imagine my life being any different. It seemed the Germans let me be. Only once in a while, a Wehrmacht soldier stopped for medical advice. I never refused helping them because I didn't want to be reported. After all, as a doctor, I am obliged to help everyone in need, even the enemy. But I can't say that my stomach didn't churn every time I did it.

Just when I began to believe that they would leave me alone, I was paid a visit by Gestapo, who offered for me to work exclusively as their doctor. I thanked them for their consideration and promised to give an answer soon. The same day, I told my secretary and nurse to never come back. I abandoned my practice and moved to another flat.

Now, I'm walking streets in the faded clothes of a laborer, in my pocket forged papers for the name of Jan Masialski. Now, I have no purpose.

I pause. I can't take my eyes off a pretty blonde in a red gown who sits in a fancy restaurant with a man dressed in German uniform. She laughs and I'm stunned to realize I know her. Anna. The fabulous actress and my sister's dear friend. I can't believe the Anna I once knew now enjoys expensive wine and fancy food, while innocent blood stains the streets of Warsaw. Just a glance through the restaurant's window makes me feel like I'm standing between two different worlds.

I want to break the glass and drag her out by her hair. I want to wash off that red lipstick from her lips. I want to spit in her face. It takes all of my resolve to contain my boiling blood. People like her aren't worth my anger. I resume walking while my heart aches. I should not have expected any better from her. When I met her for the first time in The Royal Baths Park, she seemed to believe in the goodness of Hitler. I thought she was naïve, but today I witnessed her devotion to the Nazis. It's sad how war has changed some people. I must warn Wanda.

Just when I'm about to turn into Bonifaterska Street, an interesting scene catches my eye. A red-haired boy holds a can of paint in his hand and works on the last letter of a sign: *Deutschland Kaput*. Behind him, Felek, a dark-blond boy I've known so many years, whistles and shakes his head in obvious admiration. It seems that for a moment Felek has forgotten that he's on duty and fails to watch for danger. Suddenly, a German patrol advances on them from behind.

"Felek," I shout, "*Szkopy!*" Both boys spring into a run. The red-head turns left and disappears round the corner before a shotgun can reach him. Felek leaps my way and takes Bonifater-ska. The soldiers choose to chase the other boy. I follow Felek as I'm not sure if the Germans noticed I was the one shouting. After bouncing through so many alleys we stop to catch a breath.

For a moment we concentrate on calming down our heavy breathing.

"Thank you, Doctor Odwaga," he says. He's about twenty now, though I remember him when he was in his teens. He's grown to medium height and has a solid build, just like his father's. "I hope that Jacek got away." His large eyes reflect a mixture of concern and regret. "It was my fault for not paying attention. I swear it's never happened before."

I pat his shoulder. "We all make mistakes. Besides, I have no doubt your friend Jacek was able to escape. He was damn fast from what I saw. I think we would have had more trouble if they'd decided to follow you."

He smiles, exposing his white teeth. "I heard about your practice being closed." He stares at my clothes. "Do you need help, doctor? I will do whatever I can. You saved my mother's life, even when she was so sick."

I sigh. "I'm fine. Just a little lost now. I can't go on being a doctor anymore unless I put Nazi symbols on my door."

He shakes his head and spits at the cobbles. "You won't do that."

"Of course, I won't. So quit calling me *doctor* to help steer me away from trouble. From now on just call me Mateusz."

He nods without a hint of surprise or another question. "Will do, doctor." He shrugs. "I mean, will do."

I can't help but laugh and he joins me. "I'm heading home now to help my mama make *marmolada,* jam. My ma would be delighted to see you."

"Maybe another time," I say, not feeling up for company right now.

He arches his brows. "I insist you go with me." After looking around, he continues in hushed tones, "There will be an important meeting going on. Maybe this can be a new part of your life."

I have no idea what this young man is implying, but out of curiosity, I agree. "It's not like I have anything else to do right now."

The flat on Krucza Street, where Felek lives with his parents, is crammed with young men and girls peeling apples and carrots or cutting rhubarb. They are sitting around a large tin bowl in the middle of a kitchen table. The cheerful mood reminds me of the old times, when laughing was easy. Now at thirty, I have no heart for spontaneous gestures of happiness. Everything is gray. After a short conversation with Felek's mom, a middle-aged lady with a warm smile whose life I was able to save a long time ago by curing her severe case of pneumonia, I join Witek on the sofa. He smokes his cigarette and watches the crowd. He is a good friend of my father's.

"It's a miracle you survived two years the way you did, son," he says.

I nod. "I had no idea you knew Felek's family."

"There is a lot you don't know. But maybe we should leave it that way."

I decide to be direct with him. "I need to contact the resistance. I need to do more than just hold a job."

He takes me in from top to bottom then says in a mocking voice, "You?"

"Yes, I'm tired of being hopeless."

"You would not kill a fly, never mind another human. Your goal is to always make everyone happy, to comfort them. You are too sensitive for this job, doctor." His gaze is sharp now. "And let me tell you that the work we do for the resistance is not pretty most of the time. It's not for you. I suggest you stick to curing people. They will find you in your new flat when they need your medical advice, trust me on that. You have a solid reputation in this city."

I bare my teeth and glare at him. "I can do it and I will." I stand up but he holds my arm.

"Listen, I'm not telling you this to insult you or because I don't like you. You know I do. I'm only giving you an honest opinion."

"I'm serious, Witek. Nothing will change my mind."

He sighs. "All right. Sit down. If you are looking for the resistance, you found the right person." He points to the crowd at the table. "In fact, some of these young people are about to say their oaths today."

FOUR

ANNA

31 October 1940

As I walk through the streets of the city I have grown to adore so much, I can't grasp all the changes. Those cobbled streets, once an oasis of harmony and routine, are now full of gunshots, swastikas, and Nazi uniforms. Even the old Polish drugstore on Krakowskie Przedmiescie has been renamed to Deutsche Apotheke.

October went by fast, marked by the Nazi effort to resettle so many people from one part of the city to another. Warsaw is officially split into three districts: German, Polish and Polish Jewish. People were given until the end of October to move, and today it's the last day. Of course, the wealthiest areas have been assigned to Germans, the poorest areas to Jews. What disturbs me even more are the rumors about plans to organize a ghetto. It sickens me to even think about it.

I enter the courtyard of my tenement and walk around to enter from the back. I need to check on renovations going on in the café.

"I thought you'd never be back," Wanda says. She leans

with her back to the entrance door, a canvas painting in her hand. She offered to paint various pieces to decorate walls in my café and I accepted graciously. So far, she's been bringing magnificent works of flowers and fruits that are perfect for my café.

I grin. Seeing her is the first nice thing to happen to me today. I love this dear friend of mine. "Good to see you, my friend. What do you have there?"

"I was inspired by one of the compositions Tata played on his piano a couple of days ago and I created this." She lifts a gorgeous oil painting of a field of sunflowers. "It may not go well with the other pieces though." She shrugs.

"It's absolutely beautiful. I don't know how I can thank you for this."

She rolls her eyes. "You know I take pleasure from doing it, and the fact that my work will actually be displayed somewhere is more than enough."

"You are too modest, my dear. Come on, let's have some coffee." We climb up the stairs to my flat on the first floor and settle at the kitchen table. I boil some water and we enjoy the chicory coffee I got in the black market the other day. While Wanda digs out a journal from her tote bag and starts going through its pages, I close my eyes and inhale the sweet-caramel aroma.

"We must fill our days with strong and beautiful things like poems that one day will inspire our future," she says.

I smile. "It's a hard task to accomplish, especially in today's world of destruction." Wanda is such a delicate and artistic soul. "Don't you think it's impossible to find anything positive while all this cruelty is going on?"

The way you think reminds me of my brother. He always sees dark aspects, missing out on the true beauty that hides in little things."

"I'm sorry, but the world appears to be hell right now." I

cross my arms over my chest. "We can't even enjoy the books we like anymore because all reading rooms throughout Warsaw have been closed. The Nazis keep forbidding more and more Polish literature."

"I know. But this can't stop us. There are so many professors opening underground courses. I'm thinking of signing up too. As long as they don't break our spirits, all the destroyed books can be replaced. One day." She leans forward and switches to a whisper. "I know more than you think, Anna." Her blue eyes have this earnest look mixed with a sort of admiration.

I look both ways, forgetting for a moment that I'm in my own flat. "What do you mean, sweetheart?" Does she know about my past life in Germany? But how would she? I'm sure Witek would never say a word to anyone without checking with me first.

"Witek and my father have been friends for a very long time, and they often meet to discuss things. Witek values my father's wisdom. Usually, they close themselves in Tata's library and keep their voices low. But the walls are thin in our house and my bedroom is next to it, so I hear their conversations." A mischievous smile crinkles her mouth. "Of course, since the war started, I make a point to be there every time Witek visits."

I'm not sure where she is going with this but I let her continue for now. It seems like she knows a lot and is willing to share. I'm glad she's whispering though.

"They've been speaking about you and the plans with the café." She beams. "I know you're not a traitor like you want everyone to think. You opened the café for the Nazi officers to gain as much information as possible for the resistance. Maybe even information that can be sent to London."

I meet and hold her gaze. "We shouldn't be talking about this." I lean forward, so she can hear me better. "As you said, walls can be thin."

"Please don't fret. I would die before giving anything away.

You're my only friend, Anna, and I trust you, so this is why I said something. I only wanted you to know that I'm aware of the truth and that you are my heroine."

She is still so innocent and angelic; I love her to pieces. "You know you can tell me everything but please do not say a word to anyone else. It could put all of us in danger."

"Of course. But please don't tell Witek what I told you. I don't want him to get upset with me for eavesdropping." She looks around and whispers, "He promised I could get involved in helping the resistance soon."

Once Wanda is gone, I can't stop dwelling on her words. I trust her with all my heart but she is still so young and she shouldn't know too much, for her own good. I will make a point of telling Witek about Wanda listening to his conversations with Mr. Odwaga, so they are more careful. The lives of so many people are at stake here. By knowing too much, Wanda is at risk as well. All of this must be kept in absolute secrecy.

Wanda's words only affirm how fully immersed with the Polish resistance I am now. So far things have been progressing smoothly. First, I got Igo Sym off my back by informing him about opening my café to serve Nazis. It has worked as he hasn't bothered me since.

I succeeded with all the needed paperwork by visiting the right institutions. I had to list my name as Anna von Liberchen since I never got divorced. After all these years, I'm sure Helmut or Papa have stopped looking for me, so using this name should be fine. It is an unfortunate reminder of Helmut, but as a German citizen, I found no obstacles in finalizing things and I began renovations in the café. Of course, the crew is Polish and recommended by Witek. I already hired two waitresses, a cook and a pianist. They all were sent my way by Witek and they are involved in the resistance. We want to make sure that there is no one from outside the network among the employees. It's much safer for the mission.

The mission. I've been going to a lot of meetings with Witek and another man named Zdzisiek. Wanda is right: the main purpose of the café is to gain as much information for the resistance as possible. The café will be open strictly to entertain German clientele. As the daughter of Hitler's most trusted and brilliant engineer, I know I will gain their trust quickly.

This is so dangerous and even at the thought of it, I get goose bumps. I'm not sure if I will get very far when it comes to gaining information but I know that I will do my best to succeed. My acting skills will be useful here. And, if Witek thought I wasn't capable of this, he wouldn't have asked me to put myself in so much danger.

FIVE

MATEUSZ

1 November 1941

I pay no attention to my surroundings but just when I'm about to enter a bakery on Długa Street in hopes of getting some black bread, my attention goes to a group of men in rags doing labor across from the bakery. It appears they are fixing a sidewalk. A handful of uniformed soldiers keep smacking them with their sticks and shouting in German to hurry up.

I instinctively know they are Jewish men brought from the hideous ghetto. My heart goes out to them. Seeing other human beings treated this way makes me believe I made the right decision a year ago by abandoning my doctor's practice and joining the resistance.

There is something familiar in the posture of one of the men. He wears a faded, ripped jacket and dirt-soiled pants. His long, black hair is disheveled. As if sensing someone watching him, he lifts his head and looks at me. My heart comes to my throat when I recognize him. That man with sad eyes is my dear friend and composer, Mietek. I would recognize those eyes anywhere, even though the wrinkled, bruised face looks like it belongs to a stranger.

His mouth quirks a smile but he peers around and returns to his labor. He wants me to leave so I don't get him into trouble.

My legs are glued to the sidewalk. I don't want to walk away. At the same time, I don't know how to help him without getting myself killed. Painful emotions fill me. I'm helpless. I know that if I stand there like this any longer, the soldiers will pay attention to me; still, my shaken legs would not move. Leaving Mietek like this is like betraying everything I believe in. As a practical and logical man in general, the mental state I'm in right now is foreign to me. My brain tells me to go. My absurd heart tells me to stay.

The bakery door bangs as people are walking in and out. At some point, someone halts beside me but I couldn't care less.

"Oh no," a woman's voice whispers with palpable panic. "It's Mietek over there."

Stunned, I turn her way and can't believe my own eyes. Anna. The German woman who thought that Hitler was too smart to start the war. The woman who attends fancy locals to meet with the Nazis. I want to walk away, but then, the realization that she knows Mietek strikes me with the force of lightning.

For the sake of my friend, I settle on a casual tone and say, "You know him, Frau?"

She glares at me with her chin up but nods. "We must help him."

I swallow the lump of anger that has formed in my throat. "Obviously, he cannot be helped."

She looks at me like I'm talking gibberish then walks forward with her head up and a rigid posture. After approaching one of the guarding soldiers, she says loudly in German without any preamble, "I need to speak to your supervisor." The way she does it clearly indicates she will take no nonsense from a low rank soldier like him.

The soldier's confused gaze lingers on her for a moment. "Excuse me, Frau, but who do I have the pleasure of speaking with? I'm the commanding officer here."

"Well, my name is Anna Otenhoff and my father is one of the Fuhrer's most important engineers." She emphasizes the last few words. "I own a German café a few meters from here and I need one solid man to do hard labor in there. It must be done immediately to not cause my patrons any inconvenience. I need to borrow one of your workers."

"I understand, Frau, but those filthy parasites are far from being solid." He laughs against his throat. "I will assign you one of my soldiers."

She shakes her head and continues speaking in a stable but now cold voice, "Those parasites as you called them—aren't they here to serve us? The type of work I have will suit one of them perfectly. Your soldiers are too good for it."

By now, there is a crowd of pedestrians gathering beside me.

"I cannot go against my orders to bring them for labor here and then back to the ghetto." The calmness of his voice is signal enough to me that he will not break his order. "I will assign one of my soldiers."

"What's the commotion here?" a middle-aged man with a hawk-like nose calls from the black Mercedes Benz that just pulled in.

The soldier immediately salutes but seems to lose his tongue.

It's a different story when it comes to Anna though. She immediately exhales loud and waves at the man. "Obersturm-bannführer Veicht, how good to see you." She is either a good actress or she genuinely likes this man that appears to be a high rank Nazi officer.

He gets out of the automobile and kisses her hand.

"Fräulein Otenhoff," he breaks off and treats her with a curious look, "Did someone put you in distress here?"

"Yes, actually I'm very upset right now. All I need is one of these filthy workers to do some unpleasant labor in my café, but my request was rejected."

He smirks. "Well, my soldier is just obeying orders." Then he adds quickly, "But since I was lucky enough to meet you here, I will make sure to grant your wish."

She stands up straighter. "I knew you were a true gentleman."

"Is there a particular laborer you desire?"

I'm not sure why but anger waves over me while I watch this bastard flirt with her. I shouldn't care. So why do I?

"Oh, no. It doesn't matter. The work needs to be done, so my patrons can enjoy my café to its fullest."

"Of course. In this situation, I will let you pick one that you think is suited best for the type of work you have."

"I will have my helper decide since he will be the one working with him." She turns my way and says in a hostile voice, "Mateusz, please choose one laborer. Bring him to my café and show him what needs to be done."

I show no surprise but leap forward and for a moment I walk around the poor men pretending to examine them. I pass Mietek two times before picking him, and I push him forward.

As we walk away, I hear the prick say, "Fräulein, would you like a ride?" But she must have refused because soon she catches up to us.

I'm relieved because I have no idea where the café is located. I contemplate fleeing, but I know Mietek is too weak to run away from the soldiers. We have to play Anna's game to the end. I just hope that she truly intends to free him. Why else would she go to such trouble?

"Turn into the next courtyard," she says.

After we do as she commands, we face a gray tenement with

a large sign on it: Café Anna. So that's where she entertains her Nazi peers.

The café is brimming with people seated at white tables, clouds of cigarette smoke whirling above them. The sweet and sour aromas make my mouth water.

"Keep going all the way past the kitchen door," Anna says. Then she lets us in to her tiny office with a small mahogany desk cluttered with papers and cookbooks. She closes the door behind us and without a word envelops Mietek in a hug. When they separate, there are tears in their eyes.

"Thank you," he whispers. He doesn't need to say anything else. In this emotional moment, silence expresses our feelings in the most accurate way.

"I would do anything for you, my friend. The pieces you composed for me are still my most favorite." She smiles without the guarded look she always treats me to.

I blink to chase my own tears away, but Mietek pulls me into his embrace. There is so much to say but words would not come. "I'm sorry you've been through all this. I was looking for you."

"He cannot stay here," Anna says and turns my way. "Can you arrange a hideout? When Veicht or someone else asks about Mietek, I will declare that he escaped."

I nod. "I do. In fact, we will leave now."

"Take the back door."

My flat is only a few blocks away, but before entering the courtyard, I halt Mietek in the gateway. "I just moved in yesterday, but my landlord told me there is an older lady that likes to watch everything and whose loyalty is at question. She happens to be next door to me. I live on the ground floor, so when you enter the main door, turn right." I snatch my keys from my pocket and press them to his hand. "Door number eight. Hers is seven. After I'm gone, wait five minutes, then go. The watchman is a good man. I will tell him to not bother you." I touch his arm. "Try to be as swift as possible, my friend."

It appears Mrs. Kewandowska already knows I'm a doctor and she welcomes me with open arms. I ask her about other people living in the building and she is delighted by my questions. In the end, I volunteer my medical advice whenever she is in need of it. By the time I return to my flat, Mietek is asleep on the sofa.

SIX

ANNA

28 May 1942

As I lock my flat's door behind me, I feel the instant relief of
being safe again. Walking the streets of Warsaw is equal to
climbing the most dangerous mountains. There is always this
inner fear of falling into the midst of sudden roundups, arrests,
or executions done on innocent people whose only fault is
belonging to the Polish nation.

I'm about to drop onto my couch but I pause at the sight of
Natalia on it, tears rolling down her cheeks.

I feel so guilty for forgetting all about the young blonde.
Witek brought her over last night saying that she has to stay
hidden for a couple of days until his people are sure her flat is
not being monitored by Gestapo agents. What happened to her
family brings a pang of pain to my heart. It turns out they were
caught sheltering a Jewish family in their flat. The Gestapo shot
all of them, including Natalia's parents and her younger sister.

Now, while she is in such fragile state of grief, I don't know
what to do or say. No words seem appropriate in this silent
moment, so I just sit beside her and take her hand in mine.

"I'm sorry for being in your way," she whispers. "Alek Zatopolski is sure that they won't bother coming back for me but Witek wants to be careful."

I sigh. "You never know with them. Probably Alek is right as always but I agree with Witek's approach," I say. "And I'm glad you're here as I'm very lonely."

Her lips form a small but amused smile. "You don't seem at all to be lonely," she says but then a spasm of pain crosses her face and she closes her eyes. It's like the reality hits her anew.

"Have you informed the rest of your relatives?" I ask. "If there is anything I can help with, please let me know."

"I sent some letters as everyone lives far." She pauses, staring down at her hands. "I should inform my dearest friend Julia Wiarnowska, but sending a letter to her is difficult as she must keep a low profile. You see, her mother, who died in labor with her, was half-Jewish."

I nod. "I'm sure you will be able to contact her soon." For a while we sit surrounded by an overwhelming silence. "I wish I could do something to lessen your sufferings, but there is no such thing," I say, swallowing a lump in my throat. "You need time to learn to live with that stillness in your heart. It will never disappear but with time it will become bearable to the point you will be able to go on with your life."

She lifts her throbbing gaze to mine. "I don't think I'm strong enough to move on without them. I don't even want to."

I cradle her delicate, symmetrically beautiful face in my hands. "Listen to me, my sweet, I had the same thoughts when my mother passed away. She was the only person in this world that understood me unconditionally. Losing her was like losing half of myself, and it has never changed. But I knew I had to find the necessary strength to keep going because it's what she would want me to." I clear my throat. "It was the hardest thing I had to do in my unsettled life. I was lucky enough to have a good friend near who pointed me in the right direction. That friend is Witek. He forced me to stay occupied by everyday little things and to put my whole mind into my acting career." Telling her all of this is not easy as it brings back the soreness of remembering those dark times, but if it can help her in any way, it's worth it.

"And now he brought me to you," she says in breaking voice.

"Yes. Being alone while lost is the worst thing. But even worse is overthinking alone."

She sniffs and wipes at her nose. "I should go back to work."

"That's probably the wisest thing you can do, even if for a couple of hours a day. Where do you work?"

"At the Radium Institute of Maria Skłodowska-Curie in Ochota," she says, crossing her arms and holding onto her shoulders.

"Do you like it there? I mean it can't be an easy job."

For a moment, she smiles. "I do like it. Cancer is a terrible beast but being able to help so many women extend their lives, or even lessening their physical pain, brings a lot of peace to me."

"It's what my mother died of—cancer."

"I'm so sorry," she says with a deep sorrow in her eyes.

She stays in my flat for nearly a week, until the day Witek comes with the news that she is clear to go back to her place. I don't know if it's possible to become close friends with someone in such a short time, but it feels this way with her. She is smart, gentle and at the same time strong. The fact that she devotes her life to women struggling with cancer, touched my heart to the extent of changing something in me permanently. My mother wasn't the only one affected by this disease, there are many others. That's why people like Natalia are invaluable.

When she first came here, I was determined to help her deal with her grief, but in the end we both comforted each other. She touched those tender particles of hidden pain that never stopped surrounding my heart. Thanks to that, I gained so much more strength to face this awful war and begin helping the resistance more bravely.

SEVEN

ANNA

11 November 1942

It's past midnight and I can't get any sleep even though tonight was easy. Not like other times when I had to flirt with men that were pointed out to me and then lure them upstairs, to my apartment. Alcohol untangles their tongues. In the morning, they remember nothing thanks to the sleeping powder. They assume things that never happened. But the ultimate truth is that I don't ever sleep with my *targets*.

Tonight, demons from the past fill my head. I try thinking only of my beautiful mother and nothing else. I never saw her again after I left Germany, not since the day I swore to not ever go back there. Now I still miss her so much that it hurts. Thanks to her I've built an amazing life in Warsaw. At least, for the first five years, before the war ruined it all.

I try chasing my thoughts away—I will never find sleep while thinking like this. I put on my black dress and coat. I need a walk and fresh air to get some distance from it all. I place a loaf of bread and a few apples into my canvas bag, the only food

I have in my kitchen. I'm so used to dining in the café most of the time.

I hope the fresh air and the act of goodness will restore my spirit. I slip into dark and silent streets. The curfew is in force, but I don't care. It isn't the first time I've walked outside at this time of night. I mastered being alert to patrols, so I hide in alleys and courtyards whenever they pass; they're usually in groups of two, smoking and talking. After all, they are just humans and most of the time they don't want to deal with any commotion in the dark hours of night.

I'm fully aware of the risk I'm taking but I also have in my bag the right papers, proving my German citizenship and relation to my famous father, and can always say that I got lost on the way home from a private party.

By the time I get near the ghetto wall, I have to pause in the shade of a tree to catch my breath. My heart races from the long and intense walk and sweat covers my skin.

As usual, I get near the part of wall out of the guards' sight and throw over the bread and apples. I know it is just a drop in the ocean, but I also know that for someone it might be the matter of surviving the next day. That's how terrible this war has turned out to be.

Then, I bump into something. When my eyes adjust in the darkness, I realize a little child sits next to the wall.

My pulse picks up. It's a Jewish girl from the ghetto, as she has a yellow star patched to her coat. I kneel beside her and touch her arm.

She makes a whimpering sound and hides her face between her legs.

"Please don't be afraid," I whisper. "How did you get here?"

She lifts her head and looks at me for a longer moment. In the light of the moon, it's the gaunt face of a malnourished child. Her large black eyes betray fear. She decides to trust me though, because she says, "My mama is there." She points to the wall.

I understand then. Her mother was able to get her to this side. Then why had no one come for her, to take her to safety? Once the morning comes, she will be in danger.

She retreats toward the wall and starts touching it with her hand like she is looking for something. When her hand freezes, she leans even closer and whispers, "Mamusia."

To my astonishment, a quiet voice comes from the other side, "I'm here, my darling. Is there anyone else with you over there?" A note of suspicion and worry cripples into the woman's strained voice.

"There is a lady here. She has kind eyes."

Her words pull on my heart. There is no time to waste if I want to help the little girl.

"Can I speak to your mama?" I ask and when she nods, I bring my face to the tiny gap in the wall. "I'm here to help. I found your little girl alone here. I would like to help."

"God bless you," she whispers between quiet sobs. "I paid the policeman to help us escape. He placed the ladder next to the wall and my little girl was able to climb but I didn't get a chance because Germans came and started shooting. I hid but they killed the policeman and took away the ladder. Thankfully they didn't check the other side where Rutka landed. I think she hurt her foot from the jump."

I can't swallow the lump in my throat, nor I can hold back my tears. The poor lady is still trapped there while her daughter is left alone on the other side.

"I'm Jewish but my late husband was Catholic. Rutka is fluent in Polish. Please have mercy and take her to safety. She won't manage on her own. She is only seven."

The girl looks to be no more than four. What a sad and miserable world. "Of course, I will do what I can." The moment I saw the little Rutka, I knew I would not leave her.

"God bless you," she whispers. "She is a good child."

"Listen, Mrs.—"

"Just call me Halina."

"If you are able to escape, please come to Café Anna on Długa Street and ask for Anna—that's my name. If I don't hear from you, I will come back here in one week at the same time to tell you about your daughter."

"Thank you. You are an angel."

"I'm far from that. Any decent person would do the same. I wish I could help you more."

"What you're doing is everything to me. And thank you for the bread and apples."

"I will bring more when I come back. Please take care of yourself. We better go now."

"Yes." She speaks to her daughter for a minute and assures her to trust me and that she would come back for her. The girl cries and I can only imagine how this poor woman feels separating from her only child. At the same time, I sense she is relieved that her little one doesn't have to go back to the misery behind that awful wall. That's what I tell myself on the way home.

True to Halina's words, the girl's foot seems sprained and she can't walk. Maybe it's why she didn't run toward the streets, feeling safer with her mother even if she was on the other side of the wall.

I pick her up and wrap her in my coat. She is so light. A seven-year-old child should not have the weight of a four-year-old. I want to shout it, so every bastard in his warm bed hears. *Look what you have done for your Führer.*

We reach the café without any obstacles. The moment I shut the door behind me, I'm able to breathe again. My legs shake violently, my hands tremble to the point I almost drop the girl. I realize that I ran on pure adrenaline the entire way here. I pushed my fear back and kept moving, having only one purpose: to reach the door of my home.

With still shaking legs, I walk the stairs to my apartment and lock the door. Trying not to draw any attention, I put the girl on the sofa and light a kerosine lamp.

She seems so fragile on my Victorian sofa. Filthy and patched rags cover her trembling body. "Please don't be afraid," I whisper, blinking my tears away. I have to be strong for her sake, and for my own. "And please, you must be hushed, so no one can hear you." For helping Jewish families, people are sentenced to death. No exceptions.

She nods, her eyes trusting. "Mama said to listen to you."

"Good girl." I run my hand through her black, tangled hair. "Let's take a mini bath." I smile. "You will like it."

After a scrub in the tub, I put my nightshirt on her. It was the only piece of clothing I could think of. I would have to find a way of getting a set of outfits her size, but I will take care of that the next day. Now, we both need some sleep. I don't let myself think of anything else as I'm already so overwhelmed.

I tuck her in my bed and lie down next to her. For a while, she keeps silent but I sense she isn't asleep. I feel exhausted but I fight sleep. What if she gets up in the middle of the night and tries going back to her mother? That is something I would probably do if I was in her place.

"Are you going to be my new mama?" she whispers, taking my breath away.

"Of course not." I draw my hand down her damp hair. "You only have one mama and I will only take care of you until she gets here."

"She will never get here." Her grief-stricken voice aches in my chest. She understands more than I suspected.

"Why do you think that? Your mama is smart and will find a way to come to you."

"No, she won't." Her voice is firm like she doesn't want me to keep convincing her otherwise. "Those bad men with guns will not let her. They took away my friends. On the trains. That's why Mama said we had to stay in the basement until we could run away."

I don't know what to tell this little girl. Every word that comes to my mind seems too empty. So, I keep silent hoping she will fall asleep. It is easier that way. Maybe she looks little but she is far more mature than a seven-year-old should be. War stole the joy of her childhood and offered her pure ugliness instead, putting her at the mercy of terrible people and their terrible deeds.

"Do you know the place called Tremblinka?" she asks in a curious voice.

My heart plummets into the pit of my stomach. Rumors are that no one comes back from there. Trains packed with people from the ghetto head there to return empty. These were just rumors, until one of the prisoners escaped from there and told the horrifying truth.

"No, I don't," I lie, making sure my voice is assuring. I have no heart telling her otherwise.

"Mama said that's where people don't come back from."

It's obvious Halina didn't shield her daughter from the truth. Maybe that's the best thing a parent can do for their child, to thicken their skin and prepare for ugliness of this world. "These are just rumors. Besides, you're safe here. Let's get some shut eye."

She listens because soon her breathing is rhythmic. This little girl is trying to understand what has been happening. She tries to make her own sense of it. But how can this child come to terms with things that she should be shielded from? I, as an adult, can't grasp the brutality of other humans. Since I left Helmut, I've kept a distance from people, so no one could hurt me anymore. Now, it isn't enough. Now, I doubt the intentions of others to the extent that it makes me want to vomit.

We live in dark times when a little girl's life is destined to end in places like Tremblinka due to decisions made by lunatics who think they are a superior race.

EIGHT

MATEUSZ

12 November 1942

Dressed in a long raven overcoat, Wis pistol under my belt, I listen to Felek's report. We sit in a black Volkswagen we got for the action, right across from a yellow villa in Żoliborz.

"Leszek said that the wife left the villa an hour ago with two children." He glances at his watch. "She shouldn't be back for another couple of hours."

I nod. We have been observing this family for some time and have learned their habits. Now it is time to fulfill our assignment.

Leszek, a skinny and shaved-to-bald boy in his mid-twenties who I have known since my childhood, walks toward us. He recently moved to Warsaw from Tosaki where my aunt and uncle live. We were never close, but my aunt always helped his mother after his father died. Now we need to work together as the resistance brothers.

I roll down the window as we approach him.

"He is home alone," Leszek says without making eye

contact, immediately going back to his position behind a shrubbery to the side from the iron fence.

I repeat our plan once more to Felek. "We walk through the front garden and I knock on the door. You stay to the side of the house and Leszek outside the fence in case someone shows up." I can feel already that my pulse speeds up. This is the first time I've been assigned to this type of action. I was quite surprised when Witek gave it to me. He reasoned that I must try my hand at everything, to know in which area I'm placed best to assist.

To be honest, I fear this assignment; I must kill another man while facing him. I was fine with all the prior jobs, even with pretending to be a German officer and traveling across the country. My German is impeccable thanks to my talent for foreign languages and thanks to my uncle Fred who lived in Berlin for more than a decade.

This mission, though, is different from any other. Just the thought of it speeds up my heart rate but I have to do it.

"Then you will tell him that you are from the Gestapo and have a few questions. After he lets you in, you won't waste your time: you will inform him of his sentence and pull the trigger," Felek says in a quiet and tense voice, making me swallow hard. "After that we run to the car and drive away."

"Easy." I try to ignore more and more doubts. Would I be able to kill another human in cold blood from such a close distance? Would I be able to go on with my life knowing his children had found their father dead? I straighten up. "Time to go."

Felek puts his hand on my arm. "You can do it, my friend. Make sure not to look him in the eye, and remember all the ugly things he did. Remember the innocent people that died because of his treachery—all the Poles he gave away to the Gestapo just to earn some money. Remember that he is a son of a bitch and he well deserves the given sentence."

His words get deep into me. He is of course right and it's

why we are here. If this man was a decent Pole and human, he would be left alone. "At least he won't denounce anyone else," I say and open the door with determination to turn off my emotions, to silence my guilt.

The man finally opens the door after prolonged knocking. Even though it is already noon, his heavy-set body is covered by a bathrobe and he looks disheveled, like he drank all night.

He fixes his wire-rimmed glasses at his nose and says in a sleepy voice, "Yes?"

I take out my forged document, which gives the info of a Gestapo agent, and say in fluent German, "I'm sent here by SS-Obersturmbannführer Veicht as he has a few questions." Adrenaline rushes through my veins.

His mouth falls open and I see a flash of respect in his eyes. "Of course, come in."

"Thank you," I say and follow him through the foyer to the living room. The house is empty and smells of freshly brewed coffee and bacon. I waste no more time and snap out my Wis pistol; it takes a great effort for my sweaty hand not to shake.

When he turns my way, a look of terror instantly replaces the small smile from his face as he stares at me.

This time I speak in Polish, reciting the required by the resistance phrase, "*W imieniu Polski Podziemnej skazuję Cię na śmierć za zdradę Ojczyzny.*" *In the name of the Polish Resistance, I sentence you to death for the betrayal of the Motherhood.*

I refuse to look him in the eyes. All I have to do now is press the trigger.

"But I... I don't understand," he chokes out and bends to his knees. "Please—"

"*Tatuś.* Daddy." A blonde girl of no more than ten jumps out from another room. "What is happening?" Then she takes me in, and a crying sound comes out her throat.

The thought that Leszek gave us the wrong information

shoots through me like an arrow. The girl wasn't supposed to be here. Leszek never liked me, so maybe he did it on purpose?

As if sensing my confusion, she runs toward the man on his knees, who now is weeping and saying something about changing. She throws her little body on him and settles her pleading eyes filled with tears at me. She looks so innocent and so heartbroken, ready to die with her father.

My chest tightens and my body grows hot. At that moment I know I can't do it. I can't carry out this action. But I also can't leave just like that, and I have to hurry up before the boys get worried and run inside.

"Swear on your daughter's life that never again will you denounce your people. Promise that you will never again work for the Gestapo." I clench my jaw. I sound so naïve but I don't know what else to do and with all the credit I always give to people, I can't do differently now.

"I promise," he mumbles and sobs, embracing his little daughter even harder.

"She saved your life. But know that even though I will not kill you now, there might be someone else who will do it as you were already sentenced."

I run out, feeling somehow relieved. Relieved that I didn't kill him even though I sense the man just made a false promise.

"I know that Witek will kill me, but I couldn't do it," I say to Mietek who sits across from me at our kitchen table. I run my hand through my hair and continue, "Not after the girl came. Leszek swore that the man's wife left with two children, but that girl was for sure his daughter. That's the whole story."

"Why do I sense you're experiencing relief, my friend?" He sips on his ersatz coffee for a moment and scrutinizes me.

I don't contradict him. He knows me well. Now even more

as we have been sharing the flat since his rescue. Right underneath the kitchen table, we removed floorboards and made a secret passage to the basement. When the boards are replaced, no one can notice that they were ever removed. He would use that way out if the Gestapo came. Thankfully, so far, we've had no visits from them. Mietek has been so quiet that no one ever suspects.

"At least you know now that type of work is not for you. Leave it for other peers from Kedyw. Witek will understand. He sounds like a clever guy. Besides, there are other ways to work for the resistance."

"True. While I feel relief, I also keep reminding myself that I failed."

"But you didn't fail that innocent child." His gaze is meaningful now.

My throat tightens. "They will send someone else to do it. And he truly deserves it. Because of him, so many were sent to death." I sigh and stand up. "But I didn't fail the little girl." My voice fades.

"I made pickle soup. You should have some before you go."

"I'm not hungry. The sooner I face Witek, the better. He wants to see me in an hour."

Outside, I inhale the crisp air and breathe out loud. As I stroll through the streets, I carefully avoid German patrols, so sometimes I have to wait out in courtyards. Just when I take another corner, someone from behind me whistles. I exhale, spotting Jacek with his rickshaw.

His red hair shines in the sun. "Would you like a ride, sir?" he shouts at me wrinkling his freckled forehead.

"Yes, thank you," I say and climb onto his rikshaw.

Before driving away, he leans toward me and whispers. "I'm taking you to a new location. The old one was compromised."

I nod without a word and we move along. He said compromised. I wonder by whom. One could never be sure of another hour, or even minute.

To my astonishment he pulls up right beside Café Anna. Last time I was here was the day when she saved Mietek. It's also when I saw her last. If one doesn't count the stupid dreams, of course, or more like nightmares. It's like she's possessed my dreams.

I hand Jacek some change and whisper, "Are you sure this is the right location?"

"I'm positive. Walk back past the kitchen and to Anna's office to the left." He pulls away while I enter the café. Savory smells, cigarette smoke, cheerful conversations in German, in the distance a gentle piano tune.

I head directly to the tiny office I remember from the last time. But I let my guard down only when I see Witek waiting inside. Alek Zatopolski from Kedyw, a blond-haired man with broad shoulders, is joining him. He is no more than twenty-one, even though his serious and unapproachable behavior suggests that he could be much older.

I like Alek. It is as simple as that. I like observing him during meetings when he keeps quiet but only until there is something serious to add or to assure something is prepared or planned right. For Alek, duty comes first, he is respectful and responsible. I know I could trust him with my life if there was ever a need.

I nod his way and take a place beside him across from Witek who sits behind a desk. When I meet Witek's gaze I see the emotion I least expected: understanding. I'm prepared for pity, anger and hasty words. But no, none of those come.

As if he knows my thoughts, he says, "I want you to know that I'm not upset. It was a test. I knew you wouldn't do it, and you didn't." He pauses and leans back. "Now you know too."

"You knew it?"

He nods. "It's not your piece of *kiełbasa*. You are excellent in other things, but not this. Let's keep you doing the stuff you have been doing through the last year. You are the best at it. By the way, get your uniform ready. Soon you will begin preparations for the next mission. This time in Kraków."

"Just like that, you let me off the hook?" I can't believe it.

He laughs. "Others will do it." He nods at Alek. "I need you to relay all the info to Alek. Everything you learned about Leon and his family. Everything he will need to complete the mission."

"He promised to never betray another human," I say, hating how naïve I sound. But there is no sarcastic smile or laugh from Alek.

Witek is serious too but he says, "I will not judge your faith in another human. But an order is an order. It must be done and Alek will do it."

Alek clears his throat. "I was just given another mission by Zdzisiek, so—"

"Leave Zdzisiek to me," Witek says and rises from his seat. "I will leave you both here for a moment, so Mateusz can tell you everything you need to know."

"Wait, why are we meeting in this place?" I ask.

Surprise is reflected in his gaze. "What do you mean?"

"I know the owner helped to save Mietek, but she still might be a German supporter."

He gives an indulgent laugh. "I trust her more than any of you, or anyone else in the resistance. This is all you need to know for assurance and for your own safety." Maybe he moved on quickly when it comes to my failure but he is visibly in an irritated mood today.

When he leaves, I tell Alek what I know and promise to be available if he has any other questions.

"Listen, I want you to know that no one has the right to judge you for not doing this. I actually believe that you managed to save your sanity because of that." His lips fold into a half smile.

"You speak from your own experience?"

"Partially but mostly from what other young men went through once they did it. Nightmares, severe depression. After all, it's not like killing the enemy on the battlefield. It's often taking a mother or father away from children. Doesn't matter how bad the target was or that they caused the deaths of so many innocent people, there is almost always a little one left behind through no fault of their own. That is the hardest part."

"Yes, that's exactly what stopped me." Our gazes meet and there is sincerity in his. "Do you mind telling me why you choose to do it?"

He sighs. "Someone has to. If I do it, others don't have to. Besides, my family is safe abroad, so I'm not afraid of retaliations."

We both stand up. "Well, please be careful up there," I say.

"You too."

He takes the way out the back but I linger for a little longer mesmerized by Anna's voice. I enjoy watching her. She wears a white dress that contrasts with her red lipstick and plays the piano, singing an unknown to me piece about love. People talk and laugh and the entire commotion goes on, but to me she is the only one in view. Her soft voice is the only thing I hear. Her beauty is caressing my eyes, pulling at my heart. I never felt anything like it to anyone. This woman is different from everyone else. I close my eyes and listen.

True love brings pain
True love pulls at your heart
And it's never enough to touch it
Without hurting your loved one
So, kiss me, my darling, kiss me today
Let me feel your every breath...

NINE

LESZEK

I stumble through the darkness of my flat into the kitchen where I pour myself a glass of vodka. With a single gulp, I empty it and go for another one appreciating the stinging surge from my throat to my gut. It's a quiet reason to celebrate after screwing damn Odwaga over today. I lied to him that Leon was all alone in his home but I knew well that his little daughter was there as well. It was the first step of my revenge for him causing me so much pain in the past. There is nothing that can bring my lovely Celina to life again, but getting back at this worm brings the needed peace to mend my broken heart.

I came to Warsaw looking for him. I waited way too long but my mama's death opened my eyes to what I must do. I joined the resistance just to get closer to him. I play a good friend and work hard because he must not suspect what I'm preparing for him. When the right moment comes, I will put him through the most miserable pain one can suffer. Then he will rot in hell.

I've compiled a list of his sins for which he will be paying step by step, until he dies like a dog. There is no one else in this world who's made me feel as unworthy as he did.

It all started when we were little and I saw him for the first time at his aunt's manor. With his head up, he didn't pay me the slightest bit of attention; no, he acted like I was a piece of garbage to be ignored.

And I will never forgive him for what his damn aunt did to my mother. She brainwashed my sweet mama, and then sentenced her to death.

But all of this is nothing. He took my Celina away from me. He killed her.

Now I will kill him.

I crush the vodka glass in my hand, watching shards penetrate my skin and release streams of blood. The pain brings on relief. But only this rat's death can deliver true peace.

TEN

ANNA

13 November 1942

I need a doctor to check on Rutka's foot. It's so swollen. I can't trust anyone though. Not any of the doctors I know. The chance of encountering a traitor within Polish community is slight, but still, it's there and I have to be cautious. One wrong move, and we will both end up dead.

Wanda's brother is a doctor and he works for the resistance. I saw him yesterday attending a meeting with Witek, and then afterwards listening to my performance. He stood in the back of the café with his eyes closed. It pleased me no end seeing someone enjoying my lyrics. His face told me he did enjoy it, indeed, but there was also something else there, as if he was trying to escape for a moment from the brutality of this world. Isn't that what my music is for, after all? But those primitive drunkards would never take it that way. Particularly Veicht, who watches me like a hawk every time he attends the café. Always on different days of the week and escorted by men in black jackets or suits who sit at nearby tables. Witek told me he is a dangerous man and the resistance can't get to him, but I might be able to. The way he watches me with his little eyes makes him so creepy, and it's hard to act like they do not affect me.

For the time being, I've told Witek that I need a break from bringing men upstairs. I didn't tell him about the girl though. I trust him but I sense that he would insist on moving her to a safer home. I want to wait at least a week; I'm hoping for Halina to escape and reunite with her daughter.

In the morning there is a meeting between Witek and a few other men. He insisted I join them as well as there is something important to discuss. When I walk to my office at close to nine, there are three men waiting for me. Witek chats with Mateusz while Leszek glares at them.

"Anna, my dear, please come join us," Witek says.

I take a seat between Mateusz and Leszek, sensing something hostile between them. They clearly aren't friends, but it's hard to imagine Wanda's brother hating anyone. He's such a good soul.

"We were just discussing the massive arrests in the city within the last week." Witek clears his throat, and now his voice is very quiet. "I think they arrested more than two thousand people and we don't even know the reason for it. One of them is President Wojciechowski."

My heart sinks for all the people. "That is so awful," I say.

His gaze is distant as he continues, "Professors, politicians, journalists, lawyers, doctors." He glances at Mateusz. "And many more."

"Maybe they will release them," Mateusz says with a note of hope in his voice. "These are innocent people and they have no reason to hurt them."

"Do you really believe in your naïvety that the *kind* Nazis will release them, idiot?" Leszek utters a self-indulgent laugh. "Have you already forgotten what they did in the forest in Palmiry, where they killed so many?"

"I didn't forget anything." Mateusz's voice is stern as he regards the bold man. "But the fact that you just called me an idiot in front of the lady," he glances at me, "is not acceptable." He remains calm while Leszek's nostrils flare.

"What's your problem, Odwaga? I only stated your ignorance but I see it bothers you."

"You don't know what you are talking about." Mateusz's voice is still calm even though the man is clearly trying to provoke him.

"That's right. I'm just a peasant compared to your nobility. Isn't how you always treated me and other kids in the village? Like you were better?"

"Leszek, if you want to discuss our childhood, we can meet privately. It's not the place and time for this."

He smirks. "Your ignorance, you idiot, has no end. Do you think that the Gestapo had mercy for my mother, just like you hope that they will for those people they just arrested?" His eyes are glossy. "They killed her the moment they found the Jewish woman she was hiding, on your aunt's insistence. So shut up and don't bother me with your small words."

"I'm truly sorry about your mother." Mateusz's voice is quiet now. "Still, you have no right to insult me."

The air gets thicker with every minute and I wish I'm not here. Witek stares at both men while tapping his fingers on the desk. But he still says nothing.

"You're just a pathetic coward," Leszek spits out with a challenging stare.

Mateusz springs to his feet and the other man follows him, so they face each other without blinking.

"Take that back," Mateusz says through his clenched teeth.

"I'm not afraid of you."

"Now I know why you sabotaged my mission to eliminate Leon. You said that he was alone while you knew very well that his daughter was there."

For a second his face shows uncertainty but he recovers quickly. "That's a lie."

"Enough of this, both of you. Sit down and listen to me." Witek's voice rings with anger.

Mateusz takes a seat first, and the other man soon follows.

"You clearly have some things to discuss but please take it outside of here. Also, for the good of the resistance, you must come to a truce. I'm giving you time tomorrow to clear the air. Understood?"

They both nod without looking at Witek.

"I summoned you here because there is work to be done. And I expect you put your differences and accusations aside and be a team."

For the next half hour, Witek explains what needs to be done while we listen. At the end, we all part. I sense there is no way the two men will come to an understanding. They will do the work Witek is expecting them to do, but they will not be friends, that's for sure.

I don't trust Leszek. The moment I met him for the first time, my gut told me to be careful with him. He is mean and arrogant, and I hope that Mateusz is careful when it comes to him.

That evening I watch for any sight of Wanda's brother. I don't perform, instead asking Adam to play the piano the whole time. It's not like anyone cares and Veicht isn't there.

I spot Mateusz on the way out to the back. I'm in the middle of my cigarette break while watching a half moon on this chilly night.

He shuts the door closed, nods in my direction without any hint of acknowledgment and pulls his collar up before walking away.

I clear my throat. "Mateusz?" To my dismay, my voice shakes slightly.

He freezes in place. Then with short, jerky movements he

faces me. There is confusion in his eyes. He's been like an enigma from the very beginning to me, from that night at the amphitheater. There is this softness about him that contrasts with the way he looks at me, like he doesn't trust me, or is accusing me of something.

I drop my cigarette in the bucket filled with water and rub my hands down my dress. All I have to do now is laugh and act sure of myself but I can't. I know I can trust him, so I have to finally open my mouth and speak.

His piercing hazel eyes seem darker now, almost as dark as his jet-black hair. He is tall and athletic and his stern face and steady gaze radiate strength. "Yes?"

I take a quick breath. "I need medical advice."

He runs me over with his eyes. "Is it serious?"

I laugh a little too long for it to sound natural. "No, of course not. Could you join me upstairs for a short time, so I can explain? You see, it's rather a sensitive matter."

"I'm really not qualified with women's... you know..."

"It's not of that nature. Please, come inside."

He follows me upstairs and once we are in, I lock the door.

He eyes the key in my hand.

"Please, don't worry. I just want to make sure no one interrupts us."

He nods but without the slightest sign of being convinced. "What's the matter with your health? Pregnancy?"

Heat rushes to my cheeks. "Oh, no, not that."

He is visibly relieved but still doesn't move his questioning gaze from mine.

"Come, I will introduce you to someone." I lead him to my bedroom where Rutka sleeps.

His eyes widen but he says in a calm voice, "It would be wise if no one sees her."

I nod. He guessed right away she is a Polish Jewish child because she's hidden away in my flat. Her dark hair and tan skin betray her as well. "She hurt her foot and it's all swollen."

He takes a sit beside Rutka and gently examines her foot without waking her up. "It's nothing serious. Give it time and make sure she stays mostly put with her foot raised. Also, if you could get some ice, that would be helpful as well."

I thank him and invite him for a coffee. To my astonishment, he stays. We sit at the kitchen table while I tell him Rutka's story.

"Does Witek know?"

I shake my head. "I know the chances that the mother will make it here are slim. But I want to wait at least a couple more days. Witek would want to place her in a safer home."

He nods. "Yes, keeping her here is too risky." He holds my gaze for a longer moment like he wants to confirm something. "Try not to get too attached to her. She can't stay here."

I know it is already too late for that. "I told Witek I needed a break from bringing men up here."

He jerks his head back. "He is having you bringing men here?"

I utter an exasperated laugh. "It's not what you think."

His eyes seem to bulge. "What am I thinking?"

Heat flushes through my body. "Well, I'm not a whore if that's what you suggest. Besides, it's none of your business."

His eyes soften. "You're right. I'm sorry." He sighs. "Let's speak about the girl. There is this organization called Żegota that does everything in their power to help Jewish people. I know one nurse from there who will help place the girl in a safe house where she can have a chance surviving all of this. You tell me when you are ready but I advise you not to wait too long."

ELEVEN

ANNA

18 November 1942

Days later there is still no sign of Halina, so I come back to the wall that night hoping to find her there. I want to tell her that her precious girl is fine and that Żegota is looking for a safe home for her. When I spoke to a blonde nurse working for the organization, she said that there is a slight chance that they would be able to help Halina escape. They are doing everything they can to smuggle small children out of the ghetto. The goal is to save as many as possible from those horrible camps where only death awaits even the little ones. Disguised as an infection-control nurse in the midst of typhus, she hides children in potato sacks, nurse bags or an ambulance with a false bottom.

I detect no sign of Halina on the other side of the wall. I keep whispering through the gap but only silence answers. I stay like this for a long time as it is the exact night she was supposed to be here if she had no luck escaping. I know with all my heart that she would do everything to be here to hear about her little girl. I also believe that if she had run away, she would have come to the café. What will I tell Rutka? Nothing. I will not mention tonight at all. I will let her believe that one day her mama will find her. I assure myself that if I take away her hope, I would be taking everything from her. Hope is all she has.

I wipe the rain drops away from my face and stand up into the darkness of the street. I know that once I turn and walk away, I will accept the fact that Halina will never be back and that most likely she was taken away by the trains or has died from illness or starvation. I have to move on and send this girl to a safe place where she has a chance of surviving this awful war. I can't offer her that in my home but sometimes I still wonder if I could find a way. Would she be okay while I still worked for the resistance? I would have to tell Witek that I can't bring any of the customers upstairs anymore and would have to find another way of getting information out of them. Still, would Rutka be safe with the café right under the apartment?

The moment I turn away from the wall, a sudden tire screeching makes me jump. My first instinct is to run but the car's lights blind me and two men with guns in their hands hop out and shout in German, "Halt!"

My spine stiffens at the word. Everything happens so quickly that in a matter of seconds I have no hope of escaping. I've always dreaded being shot in the back. That's not the way I would prefer to have my life ended, anyway. I summon all my courage and sober my mind to come up with a story as to why I'm here in the middle of the night. Thankfully, I have my papers with me. I need to play a silly and lost woman.

I crinkle a smile and say in the most assured voice, "Hello, gentlemen. I'm so glad to see you." I switch my voice into dramatic now while they watch me with their pistols pointed at me. "I just left the banquet at Hotel Europejski and got lost and I ended up in this awful place and this ugly wall." I know there's an event at the hotel tonight because I even got an invitation myself. Too bad I don't have it with me.

Both men in black letter jackets are sturdy with gruff look in their faces but I can see uncertainty playing on their faces. My impeccable German has visibly surprised them.

"Papers," one of them says bluntly.

I reach for my bag but another voice from the car makes my hand freeze. I know it very well. It's the one from my nightmares. It belongs to the only man in this world that I'm truly afraid of.

"No need to ask my wife for papers." Helmut's voice is quiet but also sardonic.

My chest is so tight that it hurts while my legs go weak. The last time I felt this way was before I left Germany. Before I left him. I hate being so scared like I am in this very moment. Once again, I'm the vulnerable and terrified eighteen-year-old girl. Once more, I feel no control—only fear that paralyzes me and takes my breath away.

His piercing blue eyes run me up and down as a tremor runs all over my skin. In the light from the car and moonlight I can see that he hasn't changed much—still slim and blond, his face reflects even more ignorance now. Back then, there was also this pain that I never understood, but now it has been replaced by hardness and hate.

"Of all the places, I never expected to see you in Warsaw, my dear wife," he says, as a smile comes and goes on his lips. "And I looked for you for so long because I missed you so much." His exasperated voice is like a bucket of cold water to me. He's playing his games.

Despite my shaky condition, I summon all my strength and remind myself that I'm not the scared girl anymore. "It's a lie," I whisper without looking him in the eye.

"What's that, darling?" he asks and takes a step forward like he didn't hear me.

I clear my throat. "I said I must go home as I'm very tired." This time I meet his sarcastic gaze and hold it.

"That's right. You mentioned being lost." He smirks at me

as if letting me know he doesn't believe me. "I was at the Hotel Europejski today but I didn't see you there."

"I left early as I felt lightheaded. It's why I got lost."

"And no one offered you a ride? The party ended hours ago. That's quite a long time to be lost."

"I wanted to take a walk and I sat on the bench and fell asleep. As I told you I didn't feel well." I raise my chin. "I'm better now and I remember the way again."

He nods. "Who would I believe if not my own wife? After all, I'm so thrilled we are reunited again." He sounds so convinced and genuine but that's just how dangerous he can be with his double games. Before the wedding, I was sure of his good intentions and that I was making the right choice, even though it was entirely my father's doing. But the pretense ended the moment the reception did.

"Let me give you a ride home. We don't want anything bad to happen to you. There are criminals in every corner of this city." He takes my hand and brings it to his mouth. "The destiny sent me here to protect you and make up for my old sins." His apologetic gaze is gentle now, almost as if he truly regrets the way he treated me.

I don't believe in any of this. I must be smart though and play his game. Right at this moment I'm at his mercy, in a place I shouldn't be. I also sense he doesn't believe my story of being lost. He's suspicious and he will do everything he can to find out more—to ruin my life.

"Don't bother giving me a ride." My voice sounds ice-cold even to my own ears. I can't find it in me to even pretend to be nice to him, so I turn away but he holds my arm.

"Not so fast." He smiles. "You shouldn't be here at all, so if you don't allow me to give you a ride, I may have to go ahead with an investigation. My office on Szucha Avenue is not that far from here."

The word Szucha sends a sour taste to my mouth and a cold

tingle down my spine. It's the fearful place where the Gestapo agents torture and murder people accused of working for the resistance, or in general against the Nazis. I try to swallow but it's difficult. "I live on Długa Street." I sense he would find me anyway, but he just wants the satisfaction of my defeat.

On the way there he is very cheery and tells me how he ended up in Warsaw. "Believe it or not, your father is the one that secured me a prominent position in the Gestapo headquarters on Szucha. Now I'm one of the key people there." He laughs and leans back on the leather seat. The two men sit in the front and I can see in the rear-view mirror that the one on the right watches me like a hawk.

"You didn't want to stay in Germany?" I ask in a neutral voice just to keep the conversation rolling.

"I decided to be a war hero." He smirks at me. "Staying in Berlin became boring. It was a good decision. Since my arrival here, a few weeks ago, I have already managed to take care of some of those animals."

Nausea grips my stomach and I'm unable to respond. If I'm to survive I must learn to deal with him in the most aloof way.

He gives me a meaningful look. "And now I have found you, my life will return to normal. I'm so sorry for hurting you back then. I wasn't myself."

Because of another woman named Ruth who he fell in love with. I read it in his journal one night when he was asleep because I wanted to understand why he treated me in such a cruel way. When his father found out about his plans to marry Ruth, he threatened to disinherit him. He forced Helmut to cease seeing Ruth and choose me as his wife. I know all of this from his journal.

"When I married you, I was under the spell of another woman. I gave her up for our marriage and I held it against you. Now I know that I was brainwashed by her and that she wasn't even good enough to clean your feet. She was just a dirty Jew

and I'm disgusted with myself for ever believing I loved her."
He takes my hand. "You are my wife and I desire to share everything I have with you."

He's so disgusting. I want to jump out of this car and get far
away from him but instead I close my eyes to suppress my tears.

"I live in a nice villa in Żoliborz. It needs a womanly hand."
He smiles. "I know you need more time, and I will give you
some. But not much."

"Yes, I do need time to think things over," I say, knowing I will
have to figure something out. One thing is for sure, I will not move in
with him. The moment I did, he would turn into monster again.
And I don't want anything to do with him and the blood on his
hands. He is one of those criminals. I know I can forget about getting
a divorce as his game is to get me back. But he is giving me time.
Once I have set resistance affairs in order, I might have to go back to
him of my own will, before he uses his Gestapo thugs and forces me.

To my relief, he doesn't suggest stopping by. He drives away
the moment I go inside. My head spins with a jumble of
thoughts and emotions. The initial fear I felt the moment I saw
him for the first time after all those years, is gone now. I gain
back my strength. I have to remind myself that I'm in a different
position now. At the same time, I know that he holds the power,
not me. He isn't going to play fair to get what he wants, and now
he is settled on having me back.

The first thing I need to do is get Rutka to safety, far away
from here. I'm guessing Helmut will visit very soon and I'm not
sure of his demands or how far he will push. He cannot find out
about her. If he does, he will kill both of us. Today I will try to
contact the nurse and see if Rutka's relocation can be arranged
as soon as possible, even though just the thought of separation
tugs at my heart. I will do everything I can to keep this precious
girl alive.

I change into my night gown and lie in the bed next to

Rutka. The touch of soft sheets is comforting after the chilly air outside.

"You're back," she says and cuddles into me.

"Why aren't you sleeping, sweetheart?" I ask and kiss her forehead.

"Did you go to see my mamusia? How is she?" Her voice is full of anticipation and maybe hope.

I swallow the lump that's already formed in my throat. Sometimes I forget how smart she is. She did hear me telling her mother to come to the gap in the wall in one week. The words of truth play on my tongue. I should tell her the truth; I owe her that much. But I can't kill those last remnants of hope in her. "Yes, she was there."

She sits up. "Mamusia is still in that awful place?" Her desperate voice betrays terror.

"She is doing fine though and said there is someone that promised to help her organize the escape." The lie comes easily because I know it's exactly what this little girl wants to hear, and most of all, it will preserve her hope and strength for now—something that will decide of her survival. "She sends love to you and promises you'll be reunited soon. She wants you to be strong for her, so she can find you doing well." Tears roll down my cheeks, so I'm thankful for the darkness. I know in my heart that I'm doing right by this little girl. The lie I just told her might give her the needed perseverance to survive. Without hope, our lives turn into darkness.

"Did she say when?"

"No but I can assure you she will do everything to come for you the soonest she can. Meanwhile the nice nurse will take you to a safer home." I wipe my tears. "You remember the pleasant lady that came to see you the other day?"

"I want to stay here, with you." She buries her face into my chest and sobs. "Please, let me stay with you."

"If only I could, my sweet girl. There are too many bad men coming downstairs, so you are at constant risk."

"But how will Mamusia find me?"

"I will make sure the nurse will tell her where to go. I promise."

The next couple of days are painful. I wait to hear from Żegota and at the same time I dread Helmut's visit. Finally, word comes through Witek, who now is fully aware of the situation, that the nurse would come for my little girl tonight.

True to his word, she arrives right on time. Rutka doesn't cry or protest. I used the last days to prepare her well for this moment. She is going to a new place convinced that her mother will join her any day now. She also believes that I will visit her. I was informed that I could not know the place she's going to, for everyone's safety. I know it's the sensible thing and it's how the resistance operates: the less you know the better. Still, I want to break the rules and see her again, to make sure she is fine.

After they leave, I sit at the kitchen table for a very long time, unable to move or think. I sit with darkness in my mind and a huge hole in my heart while sadness creeps all over me.

TWELVE

MATEUSZ

28 May 1943

"I summoned you here because it's the right time to proceed with our plan," Witek says and takes out a cigarette. We sit in Anna's office, which is lit only by a candle since the electricity was turned off early tonight, shortening the opening hours for the Café Anna.

Witek releases clouds of smoke and continues, "We took down Vogel only a couple of hours ago. He was on the way to Kraków for a conference with Hans Frank. He was traveling alone, so no one knows he disappeared." He meets my eyes with the sharpness of an eagle. "As of now, he is expected to be in Kraków at the time of the conference."

Anna sits quietly in the corner of the room while Witek sorts his papers on her desk. In the candlelight she looks enigmatic and divine. I would give a lot to know her thoughts right now.

I clear my throat. "What if someone in Kraków knows him?"

"Then you get the hell out of there as soon as you realize it."

For a moment longer he stares into the papers on the desk. "Listen, Mateusz, I know the risk is great, but we are well prepared for this. Even if your cover gets blown, there is still a chance you will be able to learn something valuable before that. So, it is worth the risk."

I nod. "Tell me everything I need to know." We have been getting ready for this action for some time, so everything is pretty clear to me. Still, there could be something Witek knows and I don't—something that could play an important part in all of this.

He leans back in the chair and says, "Very well, then. Listen carefully in case I missed something before." He takes another drag from his cigarette. "Our people in Kraków checked very carefully and according to their reports there will be twelve participants in the conference. None of them were ever affiliated with Vogel. They don't know him personally. Vogel has recently moved from Paris to Abwehr in Warsaw, the German military intelligence organization. He was chosen to represent the Abwehr at the conference. To our advantage, he is tall and slim as you are, and has shiny black hair like yours. But only use his papers on the train. While in Kraków, appear as him only at that meeting. Anna called in pretending to be his secretary and was able to cancel his hotel reservation, stating he decided to stay in an acquaintance's home. I want to make sure you have the least chance of being compromised by someone he might happen to know in Kraków."

"The meeting is in three days, correct?" I ask. I have been studying everything about Vogel for so long that I'm ready for this. The only thought that makes me nervous is the possibility of being uncovered by someone who knows him personally.

"Yes. You will stay in our safe house, right above Café Helga. The owner has boarding rooms upstairs." He points at Anna. "He does similar activity to Anna's, so be prepared for a lot of uniformed Germans in his café. Stay upstairs until it's time to go to the conference, and then learn as much as possible about Project Fieseler." His sharp eyes study me. "But most of all, try to keep a low profile. There also might be a time when Anna will need your help with her assignment."

"I understand." At this point I know everything about Vogel, and Anna helped me on the finishing touches of the accent from the part of Germany he is from. I have similar looks to his, and my German is pretty good. Still, the fear of being discovered makes me toss and turn at night. It won't be the first time I'm impersonating a German officer and I know how to keep my head in critical situations, but that is not enough to stop me worrying. Witek once said I'm way too soft for this war. Maybe he is right, after all.

"And that brings us to you." He turns to face Anna. The resistance was able to find out her father's address in Kraków. "I know your assignment is going to be hard on you. It's not good when there are family ties. So, I'm even more thankful you agreed to this." His voice is softer now.

She answers with a shaky laugh, giving away her nervousness. "Of course. This is my chance to compensate for some of my father's bad deeds."

"I don't doubt you, Anna. I know you will do your best," he says in a quiet voice. "Maybe it's a chance for you to face your demons, after all."

She smiles wryly. "It's certainly going to be a challenge. Do you have anything new for me?"

He shakes his head. "I have nothing new. You both need to act like you just met for the first time on the train. You know the address of your father's villa. You will go there straight from the train station. Mateusz will head to the safe house."

"Let's hope my father will greet me with open arms." She bites at her lips, a contrast to her usual sophisticated demeanor.

Witek disregards her concern by rolling his eyes and continues, "Just use your acting skills and pretend that you missed him and decided to pay a visit. After all, you are his only child."

She crosses her arms and tilts her head down while making eye contact with Witek. "My father is an old snake, so my acting better be good."

"That's the thing—no one knows him better than you. So, if anyone can put his vigilant suspicion to sleep, it's you. Spend the first week acting sweet and friendly while watching him like a hawk. Learn his habits, and most of all, where he holds his documents for *The Otenhoff Project*, and how to get to them."

"I will do my best," she says with a drained expression on her face, as if suddenly all her energy has abandoned her.

Witek's voice is softer now. "I know you will." He stands up and stretches. "Now go get some sleep. You will leave tomorrow morning."

True to Witek's words, we catch the train the next morning. I was not able to get any sleep the previous night, trying to pull my nerves under control. There is no way back and I must follow through, shutting down my fears and worries.

We arrive and board the train separately, but I enter the same compartment she does. I introduce myself and we engage in a casual conversation in German. I pass every document check without the slightest issue. The moment we arrive in Kraków, we part like strangers who met for the first time.

The whole time on my way to the Café Helga, I can't stop thinking of her. She's been very quiet and composed, but I can tell she feels vulnerable. When we said our goodbyes, panic filled her eyes like she didn't want me to leave. I sensed something else: Anna, normally so sure of herself, was now afraid. The enormous need to wrap her in a hug overtook me but I only smiled and wished her luck. We must be very careful in case anyone is watching, and I need to keep my distance from her. The way she makes me feel confuses me like hell. Never before have I experienced this fascination for another woman.

Seeing her this vulnerable brings another depth to her. It's an Anna I don't know at all. Which is that real her and which is just a mask she puts on to survive?

I know that she is ready to face her father and the demons from the past, but she is very insecure about it. For her sake, and for the sake of this mission, I hope she can keep up the act.

THIRTEEN

ANNA

29 May 1943, Kraków

For the first time in my life, I want someone to simply hug me and tell me that everything will be okay; for someone to take care of me. I know Mateusz couldn't do it for the sake of the mission, but there was regret in his gaze that made me sort of feel better. I don't know what's happening with me. I'm feeling this terrible distress at even the thought of facing my father but I know that's not the only reason for my current state.

Why do I feel such a strong yearning for Wanda's brother? He doesn't even like me. I never cared much about it. But after we left Warsaw, I felt safe with him on that train. It was nice how he pretended to be a stranger and made an effort to engage in conversation. It almost felt like we were on a first date. It felt like that to me, anyway.

I can't help but sigh as I approach my father's glorious villa, entangled with vines of ivy all over it. I wonder who was removed from it when the war started. Pausing just before entering the gate, I summon all of my courage. I can't afford weakness or sentimentality anymore. It's time to do what I do best: acting.

The gate opens with a squeak, and I follow a path through the well-maintained garden filled with white and pink hydrangeas. The air is rich with the sweet scents of honey and vanilla. My father doesn't deserve to live here, surrounded by such beauty. He probably doesn't even notice it.

I tap the door with my shaking hand and wait, dreading seeing my father face to face. But instead of him, I encounter a scowl from a middle-aged woman in glasses, her blonde hair gathered neatly in a knot. She is as tall and skinny as my old chemistry teacher, and she has that same sharp edge to her.

I raise my chin and say in a calm but stern voice, "Good day. I'm here to visit Herr Otenhoff."

Her snarl deepens as she takes me in from top to bottom. "Herr Otenhoff is not seeing anyone today," she barks at me and attempts to shut the door, but I catch it just in time and hold on to it with the strength that is slowly returning to me after the panicked haze I have been in last night and today.

"I'm his daughter and I'm going to ask you politely once more to inform him of my visit before I shout and alarm the entire neighborhood," I utter while meeting her cold eyes with mine. She will learn quickly not to start with me. People like her need to be put in their place right away or they have no boundaries. If I'm to stay in this house and accomplish my mission, I must keep this nasty woman at a safe distance.

Fury covers her face but she steps back and says in her cold voice, "Please kindly wait here." When I take my hand away, she immediately shuts the door. She is a tough cookie. But it actually makes sense my father encircles himself with the most hostile people. The only time I saw him being soft was with my mother.

The door swings wide open but this time there is a short and chubby woman in a white apron. She greets me with a wide

smile. "I couldn't help overhearing the conversation. Her ener-
getic voice is so contagious that it's hard for me not to smile.
"You even have Herr Otenhoff's voice." She shakes her head
and looks around. "I don't know how Ursula could miss that.
And look at that—his eyes and lips. Come on in." She pulls me
inside, not giving me a chance to respond. What a far cry from
the other woman.

She leads me to a stylish but cheerfully decorated room
with a floral sofa and a red-brick chimney. I'm sure the credit for
the design doesn't go to my father. He is too good at taking
things away from people.

"Please make yourself comfortable. Your father will be in
shortly," she says. "By the way, my name is Gisela and I'm your
father's cook."

"Thank you." I smile at her. At least not everyone here is
filled with hate for me.

The moment my father enters the room, I instinctively
spring to my feet. The other woman stands in his shadow,
staring at me with the expression of a hungry hyena.

But I don't care about her because when my father meets
my gaze, I'm taken aback by what I see there: a significant
amount of relief mixed with regret, perhaps a hint of softness
too. I'm totally unprepared for this. All I've been expecting was
coldness and aloofness, instead he's made me feel like a little girl
again.

"Hello, Papa," I say in a quiet but shaky voice. "It's good to
see you." What hits me the most is how much he's aged. His
blond hair is fully gray now and wrinkles crowd his face.

A smile curls at the edge of his mouth, just like in the old
times. "Hello, sweetheart. Won't you hug your papa after all
these years?"

Everything forgotten, I run into his embrace and stay in
there for long minutes.

"How did you travel all the way from Warsaw?" he asks, raising his brow.

Since when does he know that I live in Warsaw? Why he didn't contact me and force me to return to Helmut then? Could this be why he secured Helmut's position with the Gestapo on Szucha? "By train," I answer.

He must sense my worries because he says, "There is so much we need to catch up on. But we have time. How long are you planning on staying?"

"I was thinking for a couple of weeks." I try to sound confident.

"Good." He takes my hands in his. "I will have Ursula take you to the room you will be staying in." He turns to her and says, "My daughter will be settling in the rose room."

It all sounds like a fairy tale but I know better. I thank him and let the witch lead me to the room on the second floor while ignoring her huffs and puffs once Papa is out of sight. Interesting that she didn't show me any hostility in front of him.

"The evening meal is at three o'clock," Ursula says and runs her finger over the dresser's mahogany surface. "Herr Otenhoff doesn't accept lateness."

"I know my father eats early," I say curtly. "Now if you'll excuse me."

She swirls around and slams the door behind her.

I can't resist releasing a loud laugh, almost hoping she hears it. At the same time, this simple act helps me let out some of the accumulated tension. My father surprised me with his sweet approach toward me. While preparing for months for that moment, I never considered he would behave in such a way. I planned exactly how I would act to convince him of how I missed him and that I'm just a prodigal daughter seeking forgiveness. All that, to be able to get closer to him and fulfill the mission, is now unnecessary. He opened his arms right away and I responded in an instinctively genuine way. As any loving daughter would. Except, my father sides with murderers, actually aiding their effort to destroy innocent nations. I must plan my next move carefully.

The square room is lovely, decorated with rose-pink wallpaper and a massive bed in the middle covered by a rose-embroidered bedspread. Even the air smells of roses. I can't help but wonder who lived here before Nazis seized the property.

I pull aside the curtains and admire a large courtyard enchanted with little alleys between rows of different flowers and plants. A rusted bench remains in the shade of a willow tree, and just behind it there is a little swing. The realization that there were children living here before instantly breaks my heart and my breath catches. They even evicted the little ones. All so my father could live in comfort while helping to destroy innocent lives.

I turn away and smash my fist into the softness of the bed spread unable to keep my anger inside me anymore. How dare he show me such fondness while he lives surrounded by reminders of the Nazis' terrible deeds? I will do everything to get this mission a successful outcome. This is my part in this awful war. A flood of emotions runs through me, making my mind race. I must calm down and play happy, especially since that Ursula is going to watch my every move.

FOURTEEN

ANNA

I make sure to arrive in the dining room a few minutes before the stated time. Papa already sits at the head of the table reading the *Krakauer Zeitung*, a German rag full of awful propaganda. I wouldn't touch a paper filled with such lies.

The moment Ursula joins us, Gisela, the nice lady who let me inside the house, serves a chicken broth with noodles that tastes almost like the one Mutti used to make. When she returns to gather the soup bowls, I say, "This soup was exceptionally delicious. Thank you."

Gisela grins. "You are sweet." She pats my arm while the witch from across the table grunts.

"I'm glad you like Gisela's cooking. I brought her with me from Berlin as I didn't trust any of the Polish cooks. She is like family to me," Papa says. "Gisela, why don't you eat with us today?"

"Thank you, Herr Otenhoff, but I have too much to handle in the kitchen. Perhaps next time." She marches out to soon return with a second course. This time she serves a breaded schnitzel with potatoes and red cabbage. The pork cutlet is thin and crispy and the salad sweet and sour. I feel guilty eating it because it makes me feel like there is no war and food shortage outside. Since the beginning of the occupation, I've consumed modest meals, keeping in mind there are people who had everything taken away. I've made sure to find ways to share with the poorest whatever leftovers I have from the café. But in this home, meals are glamorous and that feels so wrong that I struggle with nausea.

Ursula keeps glowering at me but Papa seems to not pay much attention to her, directing the entire conversation at me. He asks general questions, mostly about how my café is prospering. I guess opening the café under my married name wasn't the wisest decision, after all. He is so well informed about my affairs. Thankfully, from the outside, it looks like I do run a successful business serving the Third Reich.

After dinner, Ursula excuses herself to attend to her duties and goes upstairs. It turns out she is Papa's secretary in his home office. At least I'm starting to find out useful information. I must learn quickly though about my father's routine, and also about Ursula's. This will help me to come up with a way of accessing the plans of his newest project that could destroy lives of so many people. According to Witek, my father has been busy working on the series of the most advanced rockets that can travel with a speed of sound.

Papa stretches in the armchair beside the chimney and I join him, sitting in the chair opposite. He raises a cigar to his mouth and strikes a match. He inhales deeply and then releases clouds of smoke.

"I moved to *Krakau* shortly after your mother's passing," he says with a hint of pain in his voice. "I thought the change of place would do me good, and I was right. It's easier to function without bumping into things we shared for all those years."

It hits me hard, remembering the love my parents cherished.

At the same time, I wonder how someone capable of loving so fiercely can harm others so easily. How can he look in the mirror knowing there are so many suffering because of the Nazis?

"I still can't believe she's gone," I whisper, wiping away my tears. "There are days when I catch myself thinking of what I'm going to write in my next letter to her."

"In her final days she cried to see you once more."

I swallow the lump in my throat. "I didn't know until it was too late."

He shrugs. "I know." Our eyes meet and our sorrows mingle. "I know, darling. She made me promise that I would never interfere in your life. And I want you to know that I will always honor her last wish."

I don't know what to say. He seems so open and honest with me.

"Before dying, she confessed her secret about helping you escape to Poland. I was too broken to get upset, but later I understood why she did it. She was protecting you from that bastard Helmut because I failed you." He stares into his cigar for a moment longer then continues, "But I want you to know that after you told me how Helmut treated you, I wasn't just going to leave it. I took him hunting and I almost killed him. The only reason he survived is because he promised to treat you better. I wanted to believe him, so I gave him one more chance, but when we returned you were gone."

"I didn't know that." I whisper trying to process what he just told me. So, he did care back then, after all. He just failed to show it.

"Realizing that I might never again see you was so hard. I began looking for you in Germany and Italy, but then your mother threatened to leave me if I didn't stop searching. I couldn't risk losing her." His voice trails away and he raises his cigar to his mouth.

Why didn't Mutti inform me of this in her letters? His words somehow help to heal some of my old wounds and they prove once more the inner beauty and strength of my mother. But now we live in another world and my father takes the dark side. Because of that there always will be this invisible line between us.

"Thank you for telling me all of this." I've nothing else to say to him. What he' s just said about our past brings a much-needed peace between us. But I am still against him with my whole heart. I know that he would never change his stand and the work he does for the Nazis disgusts me, opening new wounds between us that can never heal. If only I could convince him to turn his heart, and be a good person. I would give my life for it. But there is no chance.

"Helmut wrote to me asking for help with his transfer. I secured him a position in the Gestapo Headquarters in Warsaw just to get him off my back. Rest assured though that I urged him not to bother you. Beware though as I do not trust him. A lowlife like him has no honor."

"I saw him only once," I say and avoid his gaze. Since our accidental meeting all those months back, I truly never saw Helmut again. Now I know it's because he promised my father to stay away from me. But Papa's point is valid—Helmut's word means nothing. It's different when it comes to my father who is a man of his word. I know he would never break the promise he made to Mutti. She still protects me, long after her death.

"Please make yourself at home here. Now when you are back, it feels as though a part of your mother is back. You look so much like her." A slight smile plays at his mouth as he cocks his head to the side as if remembering her.

"Thank you, Papa. I hope not to disturb your routine too much."

∾

I learn a lot over the next few days. Papa mostly stays inside working in his upstairs office but occasionally he leaves for meetings. In the middle of the day, I accompany him on his strolls through a nearby park. Other than that, we see each other at meals. The conversation is kept to catching up, and we rarely discuss his work.

Ursula spends most of the day within the house, generally Papa's office, often late into the night, typing or performing other tasks. It's like she is glued to the damned desk. I must find a way of ensuring she is out when the time comes.

One morning I stop at Papa's office, pretending to need his help with a crossword puzzle. He smiles and says he was going to take a break anyway. His desk is covered with papers and plans, titled "The Otenhoff Project." I frantically realize that these are the exact documents I came for. I pretend not to notice and keep chatting with my father as he folds the sheets of paper and walks with them to the safe across the room. He places it inside the iron safe and locks it. Then he returns to his desk and puts the key inside the bottom drawer.

Adrenaline courses through my veins as I keep pretending not to pay any attention to what he is doing. Plus, right behind me Ursula is watching.

At supper that night, Papa is silent, so I ask, "Are you okay, Papa? You seem sad today?"

He shakes his head. "It's nothing. I've been invited by the Governor General, Hans Frank, to a ball at Burg von Krakau. Would you like to accompany me?"

Wait, is he talking about Wawel Castle? That's right. In the report Witek gave me, there is warning that the word *Wawel* is forbidden by the Nazis as they are strict on renaming famous

Polish streets, buildings or monuments to German versions. Instead, they call it Burg von Krakau or Krakauer Burg. I must remember that. "Of course, I would love to. When?" I say, casually ignoring Ursula who now glares at me with even more intensity than before.

"In two days. Let's go shopping for a nice dress for you. You deserve the finest, my darling."

"Thank you, Papa. I didn't really bring much with me."

"Of course. Also, I have a private meeting straight after the ball, so you will have to return home alone but I can assure you I will secure you the safest transport. Hope that is fine with you?"

"Oh, yes, that is not a problem at all," I say and treat Ursula to a triumphant look. She deserves every bit of it. As far as I notice, my father doesn't pay her much mind, and he is not too concerned about her evident expectations for more attention. Or is he only like that while I'm here? Something is not right. Every time he treats me with a gift or smile, she makes this face, as if she should be the one receiving the affection. I wonder if they're sleeping together.

The next day Papa apologizes for not being able to accompany me shopping for the dress but instead he sends me off with Gisela. I don't complain. I find a turquoise dress perfect for the occasion in one of the boutiques and she assures me that I look good enough for the ball. After that, to my astonishment, Gisela orders the driver to stop near the Main Market Square and instructs him to leave, stating we will walk back home.

Kraków is truly a beautiful city. I've never visited before but heard a lot about its history from Wanda. I especially enjoyed her tales about Queen Jadwiga who was coronated at the age of twelve. Even though she was so young, she became a responsible and wise queen. She was known for helping others and for supporting the Kraków Academy, by selling her jewels. But what intrigues me most when comes to her is the fact that there are many paintings of her and each one shows her looking different. In truth, no one knows how she looked since she lived in the fourteenth century. But then, even if she wasn't beautiful outside, what she left behind proves her inner beauty.

Now Jadwiga's beloved city brims with Nazi swastikas at every corner. The beautiful old city is marked with blood of innocent. Her royal Wawel has been taken by Governor General Hans Frank, the man who's been nicknamed *Konig von Polen*, the king of Poland. What a terrible joke.

To my astonishment, Gisela leads me through side alleys to the black market crowded with Poles selling food and other goods.

I touch her arm. "Gisela, does Papa know that you shop at the black market?" I ask.

She shrugs. "He doesn't care where I take the food from as long as I serve his favorite dishes."

It turns out she knows a lot of people here and they treat her with kindness. She buys a few products, like apples and kiełbasa. But what warms my heart is that whenever she thinks that I don't see it, she gives an apple or coin to children that roam around. She has a soft heart, this wonderful woman.

"How long have you been working for my father?" I ask while chewing on an apple.

"Your parents hired me when your Mutti's health worsened. What a sweet woman she was, bless her soul." She sighs and we remain in silence.

I try to blink my tears away. Hearing her reminiscing about Mutti in such a respectful way brings a wave of nostalgia to me.

"After her passing, your papa offered me a position to travel with him to Poland as his housemaid and cook. I accepted immediately, knowing Frau Otenhoff would approve it. In her final days, she was so worried about your father. I heard them often arguing about his employment for the Nazi party, but in the end, I think she loved him unconditionally."

Did she say they argued about his job? So, Mutti never approved of his involvement with this brutal regime. That knowledge lifts a weight off my heart. My mother was a good woman through and through and her only fault was that she loved the wrong man.

"When she was asleep, she kept calling your name," Gisela continues. "She loved you more than words can describe, my dear child."

I freeze, unable to move forward. I just want to bury my face in the pillow and cry. I can't stop the tears running down my cheeks. Gisela's words hit me hard. "She was everything to me. Thanks to her I am who I am."

She pats my arm. "I sensed the moment I saw you that you are like her. Your heavy makeup and sharp responses did not fool me."

I smile at her. "Why does it seem like I've known you my entire life?"

She smiles back but doesn't answer. "I don't know if you will tell your father but I know you saw me giving things to these little children. I try to help as much I can and whenever there are leftovers, I bring it to the orphanage or find poor people in the streets when no one sees."

"I would never," I assure her. "I do the same thing back in Warsaw."

She grins at me and we resume walking. "One more thing—beware of Ursula. She is a hyena just looking to make others miserable. She became worse from the moment your father took her to his bed." Her eyes reflect sadness. "She can't stand you being here and that he shows you affection."

"I've been suspecting that," I say. Tiredness overtakes me,

and the only thing that brings me some comfort is knowing Mutti can't see what Papa is doing with this woman. But there is also something in Gisela's expression that makes me think her warning is more than just a personal one. Does she suspect the real reason for my return to my father?

FIFTEEN

MATEUSZ

3 June 1943

As planned, Anna arrives for a meeting with me on the sixth day of our stay in Kraków. It's a tremendous relief to see her unharmed.

"I've been worrying about you." We sit in my room, just above the Café Helga. The last few days have been so boring but it's important I keep a low profile until the conference.

Her exasperated laughter rings out, making me wonder if she is truly okay. "Do you really want me to believe that you actually sat here the whole time worrying about me?"

"Well, maybe not the whole time." I flash her a cheeky smile. "Why is it so hard to believe that I would think of you?"

She sighs. "You are just a truly genuine man. I'm sorry for my rough edges."

"And now you're mocking me," I say, rolling my eyes. "Women."

"I actually meant it as a compliment," she says and stares through the window. "You have a stunning view on the Main Market Square and *Sukiennice*, the Cloth Hall. This is such a historic center of Kraków. I hate that they call it the Adolf Hitler-Platz."

I like that she's changed the subject, as it became somehow uncomfortable between us. "It's what I've been doing for most of my days—staring at it." I don't hide a brief sardonic smile. I've got so familiar with the sight of the unique *Sukiennice,* topped by an exquisite attic decorated with carved masks in the style of the renaissance.

"At least you have something nice to look at."

I want to tell her that there is no more beautiful view than the one I enjoy in this very moment, admiring her. Instead, I just nod and continue to the business. "How are things with your father?"

"Very good. I already know where he holds the plans and the key to the safe, but the problem is that he or his rude secretary are almost always there."

"Witek said to take as much time as you need. Actually, I just found out today that the conference has been postponed for another four days."

"I don't think I'm going to wait that long. It seems there is a perfect opportunity tomorrow." She takes out a cigarette.

"Let me," I say and dig out matches from my pocket. I always carry some out of habit even though I don't smoke anymore.

She exhales clouds of smoke and continues, "My father wants me to accompany him to a ball thrown by Hans Frank in Wawel. Afterwards, he has to stay for a private meeting, so when I go back home, I will try sneaking into his office. I will just have to make sure his secretary is asleep."

"Are you sure it's not too early to do this?" I try to hide how much I dread her being caught. The Gestapo would have no mercy and I doubt her Nazi driven father would help her.

She shakes her head. "There might not be a better opportunity. My father will be out, so I will only have to worry about the secretary. Trust me, one of them is always there, even late at night, so it makes it hard to plan to do it on any ordinary day."

"I see. Let me know if you need my help," I say, even though we both know there is no way I can assist her. "By the way, you should quit smoking. It's not healthy for your lungs." I playfully nudge her arm.

"Understood, doctor." She mocks me again and I want to pull her in my embrace and kiss into oblivion. Being trapped in this room makes me feel insane. Why do I have thoughts like this for a married woman?

"Please be careful," I say in a quiet voice. "Witek will kill me if something happens to you."

SIXTEEN

ANNA

4 June 1943

Every time Wanda spoke about Wawel, the seat of the Polish monarchs for centuries, I dreamed of one day visiting it. That has become reality today even though the circumstances are from a nightmare. Here I'm walking arm by arm with my father, the genius engineer, fully devoted to Hitler. I'm in the middle of everything I despise most.

I try to forget about the situation and focus on admiring the old castle. Before we began our trip to Kraków, Witek told me that the Governor General, Hans Frank, who resides at Wawel Castle now, isn't bothered by the Polish culture that surrounds and fills the castle, and that he has not damaged anything. So far. I fear a day when the Nazis steal the most valuable items and destroy the rest. I expect nothing better from them.

The courtyard is filled with torches and Nazi banners. Inside, the castle brims with dignitaries and officers in German uniforms, and women in cocktail dresses.

My father leans closer and says, "Before we head to the dancing hall, let me stop by the Chamber of Deputies."

I nod and soon we enter a large room decorated with wall tapestry made of silk, wool, silver and gold thread. Huge windows make this chamber appear larger than it is. But now this impressive room is being used as the castle office.

While my father proceeds to talk to someone, I look up and gasp at an unexpected view of the coffered wooden ceiling. Small sculpted human heads stare at me from above. I shiver. These are faces of Polish people who lived many centuries ago, judging by their head coverings and hair styles. Now they watch Hans Frank and his crew running the machinery of destruction.

I feel relieved when we leave the chamber. It's so hard to watch the Nazis use such a beautiful place for their administrative agenda.

"This is the largest room in the castle," my father says as we enter a grand chamber with glamorous crystal chandeliers and black and white marble mosaic floor. It must be the room where royal weddings and balls took place back then. I remember Wanda telling me that the famous tapestry from a sixteenth-century king's collection, which once decorated the walls of this room, was taken abroad for safety in 1939. I wish I could have seen it, but at least it is safe from these people.

It's not their heritage and history. First the heads in the other chamber and now empty walls in this one—this is all wrong.

So far, I don't see any familiar faces. My father introduces me proudly to his acquaintances. Unable to take the fake pleasantries anymore, I excuse myself for the restroom.

Once I return to the dancing hall, I stay near Papa, hoping for time to pass quickly. I hate being part of this event or any other organized by these devils, but I must pretend and play the good daughter, so my father doesn't suspect anything. Soon I will be free from all of this, after I complete my assignment tonight.

"Would you like to dance?" A familiar voice jerks me from my reverie. The world stops for a moment as I bask in the gentleness of the most beautiful hazel eyes.

What is Mateusz doing here? I remind myself to act the part I am here to play. "Of course."

The moment we're engaged in a slow dance, I whisper in his ear, "What are you doing here? You were supposed to stay low until the conference."

"I wanted to see you before tonight as I imagined you would appreciate a familiar face in this awful crowd. Besides, don't worry no one is paying any attention to me. The forged invitation I was able to get looks real."

I want to be mad at him for breaking rules and for taking unnecessary risks, but at the same time, it feels so good and safe again when he is so close. His assuring touch makes my skin quiver and fills my heart with warmth. No, I can't be upset with him even though right now we are both risking everything in the middle of the devil's dance.

I rest my head on his shoulder and let the intimate moment envelope us. "The turquoise brings your beauty even more to life," he whispers in my ear. "Exquisite."

My flesh crawls with sparks of electricity. But it's not the time or place for it. I need to come back to reality, so I smile and say, "I didn't know this romantic side of you."

He gives a soft, apologetic laugh. "I didn't either. No worries, I will leave as soon we are done with this dance. Please be careful tonight."

"I will."

We walk back to my father who is now talking with a tall, blond man in uniform. Papa eyeballs Mateusz and nods to him; I feel obliged to introduce them. Surely my father or his companion never met Vogel, since the man stationed in Paris prior to Warsaw.

"Papa, this is Captain Vogel whom I met on the train while traveling here. I was so pleased to see him here today."

My father extends his hand and Mateusz takes it. "How do you do?"

"Very well, thank you. What about yourself?"

My father doesn't have a chance to respond because his companion says, "Do you happen to be related to Ludwig Vogel? I know him very well as I served with him in Paris."

Oh, no. This man knows the very Ludwig Vogel that Mateusz is impersonating. My blood pressure elevates as I hope Mateusz will act natural and come up with something sensible.

Mateusz's muscles look tight and clenched at first but soon he smiles and says, "I do happen to have a cousin with whom I share the same first name." Thankfully he didn't forget to apply the accent.

"That's interesting," the man responds and they both hold each other gazes.

Right now, I'm sweating but I know that I must help Mateusz get free from this conversation.

"I'm so sorry to interrupt but I was wondering if you could share this dance with me?" I bat my lashes and look at the blond man like I would at someone I truly adore. "I favor this song."

"It would be my pleasure," he says with an eagerness that disgusts me.

To my relief it's not a slow dance. Mateusz talks a little longer with my father then he walks away. But before he does, I can feel his longing gaze on me. Oh, Mateusz, don't do this to me.

SEVENTEEN

ANNA

For the rest of the ball, I dance with everyone who asks, hoping for time to speed up. At midnight, I yawn. "I'm tired, Papa. Are you sure you won't return home with me? It seems a harsh hour for a meeting."

A smile flickers at the edge of his mouth. "Unfortunately, I must stay a little longer, but I will have the car ready for you in just a minute, darling." He kisses my forehead. "Thank you for joining me today. It means a lot to me."

By the time I arrive at the villa, everyone is asleep, or it feels like it anyway. I must be careful when comes to Ursula. She would do anything to get rid of me.

I slip to my bedroom and listen for the slightest commotion, any indication that Ursula is still awake. There is not much time before Papa's return, so I soon tiptoe through the hall to his office.

I pause at the door and listen. Nothing. The house seems to be in slumber, so I turn the door handle but at an unexpected screech, I freeze. My spine stiffens, while I'm worried Ursula will show up.

But as minutes pass there is nothing. My pent-up tension

releases as I convince myself that she would surely have come out if she heard something.

I have no more time to waste. Papa will be back soon. I quietly close the door behind me and find the light switch. Thankfully the office window has a courtyard view, so when Papa arrives, he won't see the light. I must listen for the car engine.

I edge toward Papa's desk and reach for the drawer but to my dismay it's locked. Would Papa keep the key with him? No, that's not like him. He always worries about losing things and likes to leave them safely at home. Or at least it's how he did things back then.

I lean back in his chair and try to think like him. The key must be somewhere here. And then a memory from childhood comes to me. I ran to his office asking him to play hide and seek and after a loud sigh, he locked his desk drawer and dropped the key in the pot with Mama's plant.

I dodge around the room and fix my gaze at a fern on top of the file cabinet. I glance at the door and then at the plant. This is all taking too long. If the key is not in the pot with the fern, it's wiser to return to my bedroom. Papa will be back anytime now.

I pad toward the cabinet and run my fingers through the plant's dirt. Soon enough, my hand stops at a hard and cold object. It is the key.

My energy surges as I slip back to the desk. The key clicks, unlocking the drawer. I reach into the back, just like Papa did the other day, and fish out the key to the safe.

I wipe sweat from my forehead and as adrenaline surges through my veins, I slide toward the safe and insert the key with my trembling hands. No time to waste. I must do this quickly before anyone suspects anything. I'm so close to finishing this.

I have no issue finding the right folder, the same one I saw on Papa's desk the other day. I pause for a brief moment and listen. Still no commotion. He is not back yet.

I place the plans on the desk and reach out to my pocket for the miniature camera Witek gave me. He showed me how it works and now I'm ready for it.

Ignoring all my adrenaline, I take time taking the most precise photos I can. I'm an amateur, so I'm worried that pictures will be blurry, but I get better as I go. Thankfully, I have a spare microfilm in my pocket just in case. I pause every now and then, and listen for any noise.

When I'm done, I begin collecting the plans to return them to the safe, but a sudden voice stops me in my tracks. Fear clutches at my heart.

"Not so fast." Ursula stands in her white night gown, glasses propped at a strange angle on her nose, as if shoved on in a rush, with her pistol pointing at me.

I swallow hard. Behind her, there is a door open to Papa's bedroom. I didn't expect anyone to be in there since he wasn't home.

"Hand me that microfilm now." Her menacing tone of voice runs chill down my spine.

What bad luck, and I was almost done. This witch will not hesitate to kill me, that's for sure. My head spins as I try quickly to come up with ideas. I must get this film to Witek.

"Toss it to me or I will shoot you in five seconds." She runs her free hand through her blonde hair as if trying to look good.

I frantically throw the film at her but she stays focused on me when she kneels to retrieve it. What a damn witch.

"I knew you were the trouble from the day you showed up here. I would love to see your papa's reaction to the truth about you. But I have another plan in mind." She gives a small derisive laugh while her eyes illuminate with hate.

All I can feel is a clutch of panic in the pit of my stomach. But trying to keep the conversation going and steal more time to think, I ask, "What do you mean, Ursula? Don't you have enough? You already have a warm place in my father's bed. What else would you need?"

She gives a shrug of her shoulders. "It's none of your business. Like you or anyone else cares anyway." She cocks her gun. "From the moment you returned to your father's life, he stopped caring for me. It's all your fault. But once you disappear, he will come back to me. You have no place in our lives." She spits at the carpet.

"Just let me leave and you won't see me anymore." I change my tone to a pleading one. Returning her hostility stirs her even more into hate. I count on that drop of kindness that might be still in her cold heart. What other choice do I have?

She gives a scoffing laugh. "Don't try this with me, Anna. I'm not going to fall for your act. I'm not as naïve as your father. I will make sure he knows you betrayed him, and were planning on stealing his project and when I found you, you tried to kill me. He will thank me for it because the Third Reich is what matters to him the most, not you."

She is really going to do as she says and there is no doubt that Papa will believe her lies that I was the one trying to end her life. I have never been more scared. All of a sudden, my vision goes blurry and my muscles go slack.

"Enough of this nonsense. Your time just ran out." She lifts the pistol and narrows her eyes.

I close my eyes as the gun blasts out making a whip cracking sound. I feel my heart shuttering into pieces but there is no pain. How am I still standing? I open my eyes and gasp at the view before me.

Papa leans above the limp body of Ursula, a small revolver in his hand.

He killed Ursula to save me. It all sounds so unbelievable and so absurd.

"She is gone," he says. He still holds his gun in his hand but he doesn't point it at me. "I didn't want to kill her but she gave me no choice. Even if I convinced her to spare you, she would insist on calling for Gestapo." His pained gaze fixes on mine.

If only words could describe my emotions right now, those would be damn good words. But I can't make a sound, still deep in shock as my mind tries to process what just happened. The metallic smell from Papa's gun makes me choke. I would be the one motionless on the floor, if Ursula's plan had worked. "Thank you, Papa," I whisper, unable to stop my tears.

He sighs and slumps his shoulders. Then he walks toward his desk and takes a seat. He places two things on the desk in front of him: the revolver and the microfilm he's retrieved from Ursula's body. His tired eyes fix on the folder with the plans.

"So, this is why you are here." It's not a question, it's more a statement of powerless exhaustion at the betrayal. My betrayal.

I avoid his gaze, not caring to wipe tears from my face. "I don't believe in what you do."

"I know you don't, as your mother didn't." His eyebrows draw together as he lowers his head. "But never in a million years did I suspect you would betray me like this." Suddenly his stare grows intense and cold. "You're my blood, my only family left in this world. You bring your mama back to me. And then you dare to use it against me."

"I'm sorry," I whisper as my heart pounds beneath my ribcage. "I love you with all my heart and I always will no matter what." A lump rise in my throat as I speak my next words. "But I cannot agree with your stand in this war. You are a part of Hitler's chain of destruction. It's so hard to live with the knowledge that my father uses his talent and genius in supporting the slaughter of innocents."

He slams his fist into the desk. "You're wrong!" His mouth hardens. "Those parasites you call innocent people aren't worth living. They've been infecting everything around for centuries with their heresy. Getting rid of them and their ferment equals a better world."

Any trace of naïve hope in me that my father could reconsider his stand is dead. I feel nothing but disgust as his words bring me back to the painful reality about him.

I grit my teeth. "Every word you just said is so wrong. I would rather die now than associate myself with it." The finality ringing through my voice makes me feel hollow. I had to say it.

His eyes soften as he rubs his neck. "You know I would never hurt you." His voice is so quiet and at the same time desperate.

Why is life so difficult? Why must my father, who sides with murderers, show such compassion toward me? It's how he treated Mutti as well—always with the earnest compassion and love.

"I don't think you have a choice, Papa, because I will never support this awful ideology."

"It doesn't matter. I vowed to your mother to let you have the life of your choosing." He gives me a meaningful look. "I will always honor that promise, so rest assured I will never bother you in Warsaw. Unless you change your mind and contact me yourself."

"I don't understand," I say. Is he going to let me leave and continue my work for the resistance?

"You must go as soon as possible. I don't want you to be associated with what happened here." He motions to Ursula's body. "I will blame her, say she wanted to steal my plans." We both eye the microfilm on his desk. "But whoever you work for will not lay their hands on my plans." He grabs the film and puts it in his pocket, then he picks up the revolver and the plans, and stands.

He's letting me off even though he knows I work for the resistance. "Is this a game, Papa? Please, be honest with me for the memory of Mutti."

He nears me and takes my chin in his hand. "It's not a game, my love. You'll be always most important to me, remember that. I dream that when we win the war, we will start over our lives in Germany, where we belong."

I can't help but run into his embrace. "Oh, Papa. I believe that one day there will be a better world but different from the one you have in mind. A world where every human is equal, and not treated with the cruelty your Nazi friends inflict."

"If that is the outcome, I will be long gone and you know it."

Everyone who supports the Nazis should be punished after the war. But I don't say it to him. I let us have one last moment as daughter and father. I let us, for this brief moment, forget that we are on opposite sides and that this may be the last time we ever speak again.

He kisses my forehead and walks away with the microfilm and the plans.

"Goodbye, Papa," I whisper.

"Farewell, sweetheart."

But just before entering his bedroom, he turns back to me and says, "Just in case that the friend of yours from the ball today belongs to the same organization you do, warn him to leave *Krakau* as soon as possible. Winkler confessed to me that he doesn't believe that his friend Vogel has a cousin with the same first name. He said he is suspicious, as his friend is expected to attend the conference on Monday, but has not been heard from. Winkler intends to have Gestapo investigate. But that's just if you care to know."

EIGHTEEN

MATEUSZ

Is the knocking real, or just a dream? I bolt upright as the thought of the Gestapo at the door hits me hard, in my sleep-filled state. Cold sweat runs through my body. What if Anna has been caught? Could she have given up our mission? It can't be. We had to get over some obstacles, I do trust her now.

I listen as the knocks don't stop. It's surely no later than five o'clock in the morning. I near the window and look for a car outside on the street but there is nothing. I decide to try escaping through the window as my apartment is only on the first floor, right above the café on the ground floor.

But then, I hear Anna's voice, "Please, open up." Something did go wrong or she would not be here. At least it's not the Gestapo. I exhale with relief. Since she is here, she must be okay.

When I release the lock, she scurries inside and, without a single breath, starts talking. "We must leave now. I will tell you all when we get to the train station. Please pack your suitcase."

"But you are shaking all over. Are you sure you are fine?"

"Yes, please don't waste any more time. Gestapo could be here any minute." She doesn't have to repeat this twice.

I throw all my belongings into the suitcase and we slip out through the café. We encounter no patrols on the way. The streets are not dark anymore, so we find the station fairly quickly despite being unfamiliar with the streets of this city.

"Let's wait behind the kiosk. If we show up at the station a bit later, we can pretend to be a German couple," I say.

She nods and takes out a cigarette, and tells me what happened to her. While smoking, her hands still tremble.

I feel guilty knowing she went through so much last night, almost losing her life, while I slept. She seemed so sure of herself that I assumed she would be fine. "The most important thing is that you are alive," I say. "Are you sure your father will leave you alone and not go after you? Or it's safer you shut down the café?"

"I'm sure of it. He won't interfere."

I know we will have to run it by Witek, so for now I drop the subject. "You went through so much today. You must be exhausted." I brush a strand of hair back from her frowning forehead. "Don't worry about the microfilm. You did what you could. My mission didn't work out either. The only thing I managed to accomplish is do some eavesdropping at the ball. I have some info Witek will like to hear. Besides that, the entire trip has been a catastrophe."

"Well, not really," she says and gives me a wicked smile.

A flush of adrenaline tingles through my body. "What?" My mouth falls open.

"I do have a microfilm with the plans." For a moment longer, she smiles with triumph. "As I was taking the pictures, I learned a better way, so when I was done with one microfilm, I replaced it with the other and decided to take another round. I wasn't sure if the first set came out right. So, my father thinks that there is only one film. The secretary didn't know it either."

I can't resist lifting her off her feet and turning around. "You're incredible."

When I put her down, a frown creases her forehead. "Well, if I had stopped at the first microfilm, there is a high chance Ursula would not have discovered me and we would have the same results. My father would not suspect anything and Ursula would be still alive. So, I'm not that smart after all. I screwed up."

I nod and say, "True."

She nudges my arm. "Is that all you can say?"

I roll my eyes. Demanding but cute as always. "What am I supposed to say?" I grin. "What you said is true but I think you should not feel any guilt. After all, you managed to accomplish your mission, unlike myself. Witek will be damn proud of you." I take her hand and pull her into an embrace.

It feels so good to have her in my arms, whole and safe. Touching her feels as though I now have something that was always missing in my life. I'm afraid to feel what I feel, but I also find no strength in me to stop it. I want to hold her so close and inhale her rose perfume.

We board the train at seven o'clock, sharing the same compartment. I feel a small lurch and the train picks up speed as it departs the station. I breathe with relief. Anna snuggles her head into my arm and falls asleep. I pray for uneventful travel as she has already been through so much.

There are no other passengers in our compartment but about an hour later a conductor shows up. I hand him my papers and nudge Anna to wake up, but something doesn't feel right. The man keeps rubbing his beard and staring at me as if trying to confirm something.

His face seems oddly familiar but I can't place it. But then the memory strikes me like a lightning bolt. He's the same conductor from last month, when I ambushed another train with other boys from the resistance. I recall tying this man's hands and assuring him that he would stay alive if he kept quiet.

When he hands my papers back, I ask him, "Would you like me to wake the lady up?"

He seems in a rush as he avoids my gaze, shaking his head before leaving.

I know he remembers me. The way he exited makes me think he will be back soon to have me arrested. I feel it in my gut.

A sense of dread rolls in the pit of my stomach as I shake Anna. When she is awake, I grab my small suitcase. "Listen to me, Anna. I was just recognized by the German conductor. He saw me about a month ago with the resistance when we attacked the train. I'm sure he's gone to get support to arrest me." I touch her arm. "You will be fine, just say that you met me on the train and don't know me."

Her eyes widen. "What are you going to do?" she asks.

"I must jump out." I don't waste any more time, springing out of the compartment and running through the corridor toward the nearest exit. Behind me, I can hear someone shouting at me to halt or they will begin shooting. But I charge at the train door and use all my strength to open it while the train keeps rambling and clacking at high speed. Then without a second thought, I jump out and lose balance from tossing myself at such speed to hard ground. I roll for a moment and yelp from pain.

The shooting from the train trails off as it drives away. But then, someone a short distance from me moans. It's Anna. She must have jumped right after me and I didn't even realize it.

"Are you crazy?" I shout at her unable to comprehend my anger that is mixed with my extreme worry for her. "It's insane that you followed me." I'm still dizzy from the jump, so I stay put.

"Oh, shut up, Mateusz. They would take me for questioning, and you know it." She moans again.

She has a good point. I rise to my feet and hop to her. "Did you hurt anything?" I touch her legs but she tosses my hand away.

"I'm fine. Let's get going before someone spots us," she says and gets up.

I sigh. "We do have a long way to go to Warsaw, that's for sure." To my relief she seems to have good balance and walks steadily on her feet.

I look at signs as we walk and make sure we head in the right direction. "We must stay away from main roads, and stick near woods for now. Hopefully we can find a village where we can get some food."

A brief laugh breaks from her. "Are you kidding me? You are planning to go ask for food while wearing this uniform? Well, that might work if you put a gun to their throats and demand things."

"I have a better idea." I grin at her while indicating the large creek near where we landed. "I'm going to take a bath and then change into clothes I brought. Feel free to join me." I wink at her and strip down to briefs before jumping into the cold water. It feels so crisp and refreshing on my skin. The sound of water trickling around rocks gives me a sense of peace. I gaze at the blue sky and thank God for giving me this brief relaxation.

To my astonishment, Anna takes off her dress and joins me. I laugh. "You're impossible."

She floats near me with a wicked smile. There is no other like her.

She swims closer and splashes a handful of water at me then releases the most beautiful sound in the world: her contagious laughter.

I catch her waist and bring her closer, so our faces almost touch. Every time I look at her, I want to tell her that I feel shy at her beauty. But my eyes must betray some of my emotions, because she touches her fingertips to my lips, sending shivers through my body.

"I like you, Anna," I whisper.

A smile curls on her mouth. "And what you are going to do about that?" There is a challenging look in her eyes.

"There is only one thing I want to do right now." I lift her chin but in the same moment a shotgun rings in the air.

We both jump. To our right there are three villagers with rifles in their hands. "Come out and put your clothes on, folks," a gray-haired man with a wrinkled face says.

They tie our hands and bring us to the forester's lodge no more than five minutes from the creek. The inside air of the wooden cottage is rich with damp wood and musty earth.

The gray-haired man pulls at his mustache and says, "Bronek, we must get rid of them. They reek of German scum, they must be spies."

"How many times do we have to tell you that we are not spies? We work for the resistance in Warsaw," Anna says. We've been trying to explain to them why we are here, but they just don't trust us. I can sense that Anna is on the brink of shouting at the man.

He takes his hat off and perches on the bench near a white wood-burn stove. "And that woman with the German accent is getting on my nerves," he says, looking at Bronek, the tall and massive man with shoulder-length hair. Then, he centers his gaze at me, "But you, son, you are Polish and you parade around in a German uniform. Shame on you, traitor."

"We are not traitors," I say through my clenched teeth. "I wear it undercover. If you would only listen."

A frown creases his forehead. "What's the code phrase then?"

I sigh. This man is stubborn as a mule. "I told you already we shouldn't even be here, so we don't know the code. We had to jump out of the train as I was uncovered by a conductor."

Laughter bubbles in his throat, and then he says, *"Baju, baju, będziem w raju."* Fairy tales.

"What an old fool you are," Anna shouts at him. "You feel so important. But you forget to actually use your brain and think."

The man leaps toward her. *"Skul pysk!"* Shut up! His breathing is noisy now and his nostrils flaring.

"Well, I have in my possession something that could save the lives of so many. Maybe now you will re-consider your wrongful decision. It's why we were sent on this mission and we need to deliver it safely to Warsaw, to Witek, our chief."

He grabs her chin with his calloused hand and says in this eerily composed voice, "I don't believe a word you say. And the fact you know the names of our commanders, tells me you know too much." He abruptly walks away. Before exiting the cottage, he looks back and says in a stern voice, "But whatever you're telling me can be easily verified." He turns to the enormous man. "Bronek, call Leszek over. He worked under Witek, so if they are telling the truth, he will recognize them."

NINETEEN

LESZEK

The silly girl so willingly gives what I demand. I close my eyes and imagine delving into the warmth of my sweetest Celina. Her black eyes smile at me and her touch sends delightful currents through my blood. I can die now united with my love.

But the girl's impatient and loud voice jerks me from my trance. "Ouch... It hurts."

I pull myself away and I shriek at her, "Get out of here, you stinky whore."

She scurries away like a ferret.

Why did this useless bitch have to ruin my blissful moment? That's all I have left after my gorgeous Celina: memories of her captivating eyes and angelic face. Her raven hair always shone, bringing an aura of undivine beauty to her. And for a brief moment minutes ago, she was with me again.

At the rapid door knock, I wonder if the girl decided to rightfully apologize for her coldness. No, she is way too shy to be hammering like this.

"Who's there?" I say but without waiting I crack the door open to stammer into Bronek's enormous figure.

He crosses his arms at his chest and stares down at me. "Anzelm needs you," he says in a grumpy voice.

For some reason this giant grouch doesn't like me. Like I did anything to him. "I'll be there in a minute," I say and turn away.

"Now," he barks, grabs my arm and hurls me forward.

I free myself from his grasp and say, "Fine, I'm going." What would this old fool Anzelm need from me, anyway? But when we enter his shack, I can't believe my own eyes. The last person I expect here is Odwaga and that German woman from the café. Their hands are tied while old Anzelm hovers around them. What the hell?

I shake off my surprise and summon myself to act neutral, like I don't know them. I will not let this opportunity for revenge slide between my fingers. The moment I've been waiting for has finally arrived. How ironic that Witek sent me away from Warsaw obviously favoring Odwaga, and he flew into my trap like a diseased fly.

I must play this fool Anzelm and convince him to release that rake into my hands. If he's holding them, it means he suspects them of treachery. I will deal with Witek later. Now there is only one thing I must do to finally fulfill my promise of vengeance.

TWENTY

MATEUSZ

I never thought that I would be happy seeing Leszek. The boy hates my guts but as a resistance member he has to tell the truth, which will save our lives. After all, Witek values him because of his devotion.

The moment his bald head appears in the door frame, I exhale with relief even though he says nothing when he notices us.

"Leszek, please come in, my friend," the older man says and points at us. "These two say they are working under your former commander in Warsaw. Do you know them?"

He scans over us and, to my relief, there is no trace in his face of the distaste he treated me with.

He shakes his head. "I don't know them. They certainly do not work for Witek." His words feel like a stab in the back.

"What the hell, Leszek. Tell them the truth or you will regret this," I say through my clenched teeth. What a traitor. Only now do I realize the true extent of his hatred toward me.

He doesn't pay me any attention but faces the older man. "I'm not sure who these people are but they certainly do not belong to the resistance in Warsaw. If I was you, I would get rid of them as soon as possible, especially now they know about Witek. We cannot compromise him."

"What's wrong with you?" Anna says, her eyes seem to bulge. "Witek will make you pay for this, traitor."

"It's clear that they both are German spies then," the older man says. "Just like I thought. Bronek, take them behind the barn and get rid of them."

Leszek gives a cocky smile and claps the man on the back. "This is the right decision."

"Don't listen to him. He's doing this because he hates me. Please send for someone else in Warsaw. They will confirm our story," I say feeling like I'm going to choke.

"We are done here," the older man says, narrowing his eyes.

"No, no, no. This isn't happening," Anna whispers, squeezing her eyes shut. "Do something or they will kill us." Her darting gaze is on me now.

"For the memory of your mother, Leszek, tell the truth." I fail to remove the pleading from my voice but I must do every-thing to save us.

He just snarls at us and steps out of the cottage. The whole time, he showed no indication that he knew us at all. Nothing that would alarm the older man, nothing to make him doubt Leszek's story. I never thought he could be capable of such treachery. I never suspected he would want my death so badly.

Then the chest-squeezing realization that they are really going to kill us hits me. Our own people. And there are no argu-ments that get through to them. The old man is so sure about our guilt that he won't listen at all. I don't know what to do anymore. If we try to run, they will surely shoot us anyway.

I inhale the fresh, clean air of the forest while they lead us behind a wooden shack. These are probably the last breaths I will take.

"So that's it?" Anna says and glares at me. "You're not going to do anything. You're just letting them shoot us?"

"What am I supposed to do?" I try to keep my anger at bay but she is really getting on my nerves.

She gives an exasperated laugh. "Of course, the gentle Mateusz who would not harm a fly. Maybe you should thank them that they are kind enough to shoot us."

"Good to know what you really think of me," I shout back at her. "It's funny how you can't do anything but expect me to come up with a miracle."

"Forget it. Do what you are best at—accept your doomed fate." We glare at each other for a long moment while the men push us into a tall grass behind the old barn.

I lean closer to her. "Let's run and die with dignity," I whisper but at the same time someone shouts at us, voice full of panic, "Stop this. They are our people."

Jacek, the rikshaw boy from Warsaw, charges at us and spreads his hands as if to stop the man from firing his rifle. His breathing is heavy. Bronek hesitates at first but eventually lowers his weapon. An unexpected release of tension washes over me.

The gray-haired Anzelm bolts toward us. "Jacek, what is the meaning of this?"

After catching his breath, Jacek says, "It's all good, Anzelm. These are Witek's people. You can untie them."

"But Leszek said they don't work for Witek." He looks around but there is no sight of Leszek. "Where is he?"

Jacek frowns. "The same Leszek sent here by Witek last month?"

"Yes, the same one." He rubs his chin now.

"I'm not sure why he would do that. He used to work closely with both of them." He turns our way and grins, "How good I arrived just in time with a message for Anzelm. I heard you shouting and recognized your voices. What are you doing here?"

"We had an emergency situation on the way back from Kraków but we were mistaken for traitors," Anna says, glaring at Anzelm.

TWENTY-ONE

ANNA

9 June 1943, Warsaw

A couple of days after my return from Kraków, Witek visits me in my apartment above the café. He seems quieter than usual.

"What is it, Witek? I can see something bothers you," I say and take a sip of my ersatz coffee. It's still early morning, so that's all I can stomach so far today.

He puts down his mug and sighs. "I'm worried about Mateusz. He hasn't been showing up for meetings since your return from Kraków, and Felek says he got drunk on vodka the other day. While they were drinking, Mateusz didn't utter a single word to him."

My throat feels scratchy as I say, "Mietek's death hit him really hard." I was sitting right next to him when Jacek told him about it on our journey home. There was a night raid in the building where Mateusz lived. Mietek must have been asleep when the Gestapo entered the flat; he didn't have enough time to run into the hideout Mateusz prepared for him. Felek found his body on the floor in the kitchen.

Mateusz took the news without a word. He didn't utter a single sound on our way to Warsaw. It was as if he closed himself to the entire world. That is when I saw him last. The terrible news hit me hard too. I adored Mietek and would have done everything to keep him safe. He was such a dear friend to me, long before the war.

"I know. I tried talking to him but he just stared at me the whole time, saying nothing. Something is wrong with him and I don't know how to help him."

"He just needs time to learn to live with it. After all, he lost someone so dear to him."

"I don't know. I'm just worried that because of the mental trauma he is in, he might do something stupid." He takes my hand in his. "Would you try talking to him? Maybe he will listen to you."

I look away and shrug. "I doubt it, but I will try."

He squeezes my hand. "Thank you, my friend. I found him a new flat in Żoliborz. The other one wasn't safe to return to. Who knows if the Gestapo weren't looking specifically for Mateusz?"

I nod. "I will go soon."

"Remind me later to give you the exact address.

"I will. At least we don't have to worry about Leszek anymore, I suppose?"

"He can't be found. But I can assure you that once we get him, he will pay for his treachery."

"Why was he even working with that man Anzelm and not here?"

"I sent him outside Warsaw because I saw he kept provoking Mateusz." He sighs. "I thought separating them would solve things..."

"If not for Jacek, he would have got us killed."

～

True to my word, I take a tram to Żoliborz the same evening. I asked Adam, the piano player, to watch over the café. He did such a wonderful job while I went to Kraków. He also told me that Helmut came asking for me multiple times. As per my instructions, Adam informed him that I went to visit my relatives but didn't say where.

It makes me nervous knowing that Helmut had a sudden urge to see me. Since our initial encounter that night last year, he hasn't shown up once in my café. But the moment I left, he decided to visit. Was it coincidence or did he know very well that I left Warsaw? Is he spying on me? I must tell Witek about it and be more careful. With all the resistance people coming to meeting at the café in the mornings or late nights, Helmut might start suspecting something.

I chase my thoughts away and enter a courtyard to Mateusz's new flat. He lives on the first floor, so I locate number ten and knock at the door in the pattern we all use under Witek's command: three single taps and two soft conks. I wait a few minutes, look both ways and repeat the same pattern once more.

This time the door opens, so I go in. He locks it after me and without a word wanders away and lies down on the beaten sofa that has seen better days.

I take the room in and realize that there are only a few other items in here, all in the same shape as the sofa—old and battered. "How are you, Mateusz?" I ask.

He closes his eyes and rubs his stubble. It's the first time I've seen him unshaven.

I take a seat next to the sofa on the floor. "That's what I thought. I heard you don't talk to anyone anymore, huh?" After long minutes of silence, I sigh. "Fine. I will be back tomorrow with Wanda. I'm sure you will talk to her." I get up and take a step away, but he holds my arm.

"Stop your games, Anna. Do not bother my sister or my parents. They're safer far away from me, that's why I haven't visited them for months. I don't want the Gestapo to bother them because of me. Understand?"

His eyes reflect fear. Fear for people he loves the most. "Then talk to me," I whisper.

He takes his hand away. "I can't. It hurts too much to even talk."

I kneel beside him and squeeze his hand in mine. "You don't have to be all alone with this. I'm sharing the same pain, as I cherished Mietek's friendship. Cry with me and take some of that heavy load off your heart. I promise it will help a little."

"They shot him like a rat. Those barbarians," he whispers, sobbing. "He was so talented and such a gentle soul. He didn't deserve to go like that." His sobs intensify. I wrap him in a tight hug and he weeps into my chest. "And I wasn't there when he needed me the most."

For a long moment we cry together, our tears mingling like drops of rain. In that moment, something ultimately shifts between us. He is not just another man from the resistance anymore. He is my friend now. It's not easy to expose yourself in front of others, and he did it today with me. He opened his vulnerability to me. This amazing man with heart so huge that it's impossible for him to survive in this awful world.

We stay in our embrace, long after all tears are dry. Silence suits the moment so perfectly.

"Thank you," he says. "I do feel better."

"Every pain needs time to heal. Yours will too. Mietek will stay in your heart forever. But you must move on to be able to keep going in this dark world we live in."

Red lines cover the whites of his eyes.

"You're very tired. Get a good night's sleep and I want to see you tomorrow at the café."

"Thank you," he whispers. His warm fingers brush my cheek while his hot gaze sweeps over me.

I close my eyes taking this moment in, enjoying his soft touch.

"Don't let me kiss you just because you feel pity for me," he says, his voice sensual.

I open my eyes and whisper, "It's not pity I feel."

His intense stare reflects all the unspoken emotion that has been building between us for so long now. "Tell me, Ania, what do you feel? Does this scare you as much as it does me?"

Hearing him saying my nickname in the Polish way brings so much pleasure. "I don't even know how to name what I feel. But I assure you it's not pity. And yes, it scares me like hell because I don't understand it."

He tilts my chin up and crushes his mouth into mine while he runs his hand back and forth my back.

He is far from gentle. His hungry mouth devours me and urges me to respond. When I do, our tongues meet and the kiss intensifies, running tingles up and down my spine. The greedy way he kisses me is just perfect. It reflects my hunger for him as well. I want more, and more, and more.

I keep running my hand through his soft hair while his hand travels down to my thighs. I want him more than I ever wanted any other man. The truth is, from the very first time we met, I couldn't pretend to be someone else in front of him. The earnest way he always looks at me, makes me act like the old, shy Anna I was before the war. Before Helmut.

When he lifts his mouth from mine, my heart beats so fast that I feel breathless. I bury my face into his chest, wanting to feel him even closer. I can hear how frantic his heart is beating.

"I can't get enough of you," he says while running his hand through my hair. Then his expression changes. "But we shouldn't complicate things."

His words bring so much disappointment, I can't help but

sigh heavily. "Aren't they already complicated?" I ask, trying to hide my emotion.

"Yes. But we need to focus on the resistance right now and the last thing we need is distraction. What happened to Mietek almost brought me down." He lifts my chin. "If anything happened to you because of me, I would never forgive myself. You play a dangerous game every day, Anna, and you need all your focus."

I want to tell him how wrong he is and that there is nothing more important in life than love, but at the same time, I don't know if what I feel for him is even true love. I don't know what he feels. Maybe he kissed me because he had a weak moment and needed a little comfort?

"And the fact that you have a husband doesn't help either."

So that's what really bothers him. I move away from him, trying to silence the pain his last words caused. "You mean the man from whom I ran away almost ten years ago because he treated me so badly? The same man who some call a Butcher of Szucha?" I force a sardonic laugh. "Of course, you're talking about him because I don't have any other husband."

"Ania," he whispers hoarsely and touches my arm.

I spring away from the sofa and leap toward the door. "Do not call me that anymore." I walk out.

I resolve to walk back home. I have so much pain in me that I can't stomach sitting next to others on the streetcar. Of course, Mateusz doesn't want to get involved with a married woman. Even Wanda told me a while back that her brother is conservative, who enjoys the old ways; he'd want to get married before making love. How could I think he'd break his rules and get romantically involved with a married woman?

I don't blame him for pulling away. Isn't his old-fashioned chivalry what I like so much about him? It's better he showed his cards now before we got more involved. It would hurt much more then. Still, for some reason it bothers me more than it should. I'm just a hopeless romantic deep down and Mateusz is the one that was able to awaken that part in me again.

I tell myself that it's all for the good, that it's better it all ended before love had a chance to bloom. I must go back to my acting at the café, forgetting the tenderness I felt today when he kissed me. He is the wrong person for me, at the wrong time.

TWENTY-TWO

ANNA

The moment I enter my flat, I feel pain in my throat, and I try not to cry. Self-pity is not going to help, so the most sensible thing is to just move on. A good night's sleep will restore my spirit and give me energy to face a new day of danger.

I switch the light on, relieved that tonight there are no issues with electricity. One never knows for how long though. I take off my shoes and head toward my bedroom when a familiar chilling voice stops me dead in my tracks.

"Why so late?"

I spin around, almost knocking down a lamp while my stomach hardens. "How did you get here?"

But my stern voice has no effect on him because he smiles in self-amusement. "Well, it wasn't difficult to prove that I'm your husband, my dear. People living here are very respectful unlike yourself."

I grind my teeth. "Don't ever come here like this," I say, inserting venom into my stare.

He chuckles. "You're too harsh, my sweet." He treats me with a warning glare. "But I'm willing to overlook it this time too as long as you correct your attitude."

It takes a lot out of me not to smack or shake him. How I hate him. I force myself to smile despite everything in me burning with distaste. We both know that he could arrest me for no reason if he wished to. "Please forgive me. I'm just worrying that if you could get in, someone else could too."

"You can feel safe. The reason I'm here is because everyone knows I'm your husband." He smirks. "Not to mention my position in this city."

I want to laugh in his face and throw him out but I nod and take a seat on the sofa while he follows suit. "Perhaps we can plan a better time for your visit. I'm exhausted right now."

"I'm afraid you will run out on me again. You were gone for so long I began worrying. I was about to start my own investigation."

"I paid Papa a visit," I say, knowing it will stop all his speculations. "He told me that you vowed to keep your distance from me." I meet his gaze with my own intense stare.

He utters a malicious laugh a moment too long, then he grabs my arm getting so close that I can smell the liquor on his breath. "No one has the power to force me to neglect my wife, not even your father." He releases his painful grip. "Besides, he wasn't serious."

So that's his game: to eventually disregard Papa's words and turn it into a silly joke. "It's not what he told me."

"When he learns that all I want is to protect you, he will change his mind. Either way, it doesn't matter because you're my wife and nothing will ever change that."

"You didn't care back when you..." My words trail off as I realize this discussion is pointless. Too many bad memories. He will never understand it anyway, and at this point, I don't want him to. I just want him to leave me alone. If I could, I would run from him once more, but these are even more difficult times. The problem of our marriage must be resolved in an entirely different manner.

"I'm terribly sorry for the way I treated you." His tone and manner have changed, but there is still an edge of malice. "I will do everything to make up for my poor behavior toward you back then."

He was always good with words but I don't buy his act. I edge toward the window. I can't stand being so close to him. "Stop it, Helmut. We both know you never loved me and there is no reason for that to change now." I decide to put all my cards on the table. I'm exhausted with his twisted games.

"Who cares about love? It's the most useless thing. What's important is that couples have the same principles and support each other in their accomplishments. I'm in great awe of you, Anna. Even though you live in this hellish place with these primitive people, you found a way to support our Fuhrer, entertaining his warriors. The mental health of a soldier is as important as the physical. You're a gold standard for other German women, and I'm so proud to call you mine."

I force myself to sustain my nausea at his pathetic speech. Oh, God, how I'm proud not to be the woman he just described with such pride. What sick pride. "You didn't think this way about love back in old times." I turn to face him. "Once, you loved with all your heart, Helmut, and no amount of your lies will prove otherwise."

For a quick moment, a dark emotion shows in his eyes, but it's gone as quickly as it appeared. "I don't know what you are talking about."

"You see, back then, as naïve and young as I was, I still tried understanding your motives for treating me the way you did. So, I read your diary."

He averts his gaze and says in a quiet but dangerous voice, "You had no right."

"You had no right to hit me or degrade me, but you still did it."

His face is like an iron now and I can see he is fighting something within himself.

"You loved Ruth so dearly. You even said that she brought out the good side in you. I couldn't understand why you didn't fight for her and refuse to marry me."

He springs off the sofa and once more gets too close to me. "I had to make a choice between sharing Ruth's poverty and leaving behind everything I knew, or a wealthy life without her." His poisonous laugh stirs uneasiness in my stomach. "You don't even know how glad I am that I chose the second. I was so blind back then. I let emotions cloud my judgment. I could never be one of them."

This man is a pathetic marionette. He put his comfort before love, and now he punishes other people for that. Then Witek's words from years back ring in my mind: "He betrayed his lover, who was Jewish."

"What happened to her? What happened to Ruth?"

"What do you think happened to most of Jews in Germany? They got what they deserved."

"What happened to Ruth, the woman you called the love of your life?" I demand, my voice bitter.

"I had to do what every good German should," he says but this time he fails to mask the pain in his eyes. "I gave them the chance to survive. They would have been hunted down anyway, but thanks to me they got at least a chance to stay alive in the camp."

I give a shaky laugh. "So, you betrayed her? You put her in the hands of the Gestapo?"

"Enough, Anna. You know it's the only choice I had. Besides, it's all in the past now. Even if they still live, they will just be slaves to people like us."

An overwhelming realization washes over me, bringing heaviness to my heart. "They?"

He pounds his fist into the wall. "Damn, yes. I had a little bastard with her. But you can be assured they mean nothing to me and most likely are gone anyway. You are all I have."

The disgust I feel for him paralyzes me. I want to spit in his face, or better, find my pistol and shoot him. For the first time in my life, I could kill another. I'm scared at all the hate filling my heart. I hoped there might be a softer side to him but whatever Ruth awakened in him back then wasn't strong enough; it has turned to poison.

I know that I've already pushed him too hard and if I don't stop, he will suspect I don't share his views at all. So, I force a fake smile once more and say, "You did the right thing." I hate myself for these words but I can't risk his anger and higher chance of my cover being blown.

"I know I did. I never regretted my decision. I let that woman brainwash me and make me believe in love. But it was all an illusion. She was only after my wealth. She used me to secure a comfortable life. She used me, so she could survive the war while others like her were doomed. Now I know everything I felt for her was wrong and she had to pay the price of her kind."

It's clear he believes in everything he says, or he wants to believe it. It's like he is trying to convince himself. "I see," I say, feeling so drained.

"Every time I deal with one of those Polish bandits, I feel a raw power. I'm finally being true to myself, to everything I believe in. So, you see, my dear wife, that little episode from my past means nothing. Everything I wrote in that journal was naïve and pathetic, and I knew no better back then. Now I know the ultimate truth."

He tortures other people to feel better about himself—he is the biggest sadist on Szucha. He doesn't even hide it; he is so proud of it. I can't believe he ever truly loved poor Ruth or their child. He is only capable of loving himself. What a psychopath. And now, I'm the one stuck with him.

TWENTY-THREE

MATEUSZ

10 June 1943

Four taps, pause, three knocks. One of our people. I open the door and let Jacek in. His cheeks and eyes are red as he settles his darting gaze on me.

"What's so important at seven o'clock in the morning?" I ask, hoping it's just one of Witek's messages in regard to today's meeting.

"Gestapo arrested Felek about three hours ago. We are not sure if someone ratted him out or if it was just coincidence," he says and wipes sweat from his forehead.

A sudden, overwhelming sensation of dread settles in the pit of my stomach. "Are you sure?"

He sighs. "I wish I was wrong. Felek is a good friend," he says in an emotion-choked voice.

I swallow hard and put my hand on his arm. "Don't worry, boy. Rest assured we will do everything to get him out."

His eyes widen like he doesn't believe me. "They took him to Pawiak."

I'm determined not to waste another minute. Time is gold

right now as the Gestapo are quick to torture, especially if the victim doesn't give them any information. I doubt Felek will supply them with anything. He might be skinny and small but he doesn't lack stamina and bravery. Most of all, he is stubborn like a mule. He won't tell them a thing. But I don't want to even think about what they will put him through. The longer he is in their hands, the less chance he has to survive.

"Any word from Witek?" I ask while putting my shoes on.

"He says not to go to Café Anna as it might be compromised as well."

"Are you available to drive me to his flat now?"

"I just came from there, but yes, that is no issue."

"Something to drink?" Witek asks as we take seats at his kitchen table.

I shake my head and get straight to the point. "Jacek told me about Felek."

His face grows somber. "We don't know details, just that he was taken to Pawiak. I already ordered for our magazines with ammunition to be moved to new locations and I need you to go to Zoliborz to help with that. Also, no more meetings at Café Anna, not until we know it isn't compromised."

"You know very well that Felek won't talk," I say, my frustration growing.

"I agree but we must be careful. The truth is that none of us know how we would behave under torture." He drills his gaze into mine. "And those bastards don't joke around."

I get up and spread my hands on the wall. "You don't need to remind me. They will probably have him at Szucha today. We have no time to waste."

He jerks his head up to search my face. "Please don't tell me that you hope to get him out of there? Unless, thanks to sheer luck, they release him, there is nothing we can do." He points his finger at me. "And you know it."

"We need to try at least. We must do that much for him."

He takes out a cigarette and lights it with a match. After exhaling clouds of smoke, he says, "If only it was that easy, so many people would be alive now. We don't even dare to try and help the top resistance ranks to escape. Once someone is classified as a political prisoner, those monsters act quickly and take extra measures. And they are capable of killing hundreds in retaliation of any attempts of ours."

Of course, he is right but I can't give up on Felek. "The action in March was successful though." I give him a challenging look. "I don't know details but I heard that the man was freed while on the way from Szucha to Pawiak."

"He died a few days later. No doctor could help him." His voice trails away, a flicker of sadness crossing his face. "And they have taken extra steps for security since then."

I didn't know that part of the story. But if it could be done then it can be done now. And it doesn't mean they will retaliate again. "That's why we can't waste any more time," I say in a quiet voice. "Listen, I'm only asking you to give me a few boys from Kedyw. That's all."

He sighs. At least he's considering it. "It's not that easy. Besides, it's not my decision to make. I would have to go through Zdzisiek and the others."

"Please, at least try. Felek is more than just a friend. I've already lost Mietek, and now Felek is in danger." I wasn't there when Mietek needed me but I feel that there is still something I can do for Felek. Nothing is going to stop me from at least trying.

"I know he is. Go help moving the ammunition from Żoliborz. I will find you as soon I have any news."

≈

I do as he says through most of the day, then I go to my flat, praying to hear from Witek. I've hope in me that there is still a way of saving my young friend.

At five o'clock in the afternoon, Witek comes over with Alek Zatopolski. I take it as a good sign that he is not alone.

"I still think this is pure madness and it's not going to work," Witek says and drops to the sofa. "But, if you're still up to it," he points at Alek who relaxes against the wall with hands in his pockets, "Alek and a couple of other boys from Kedyw will help you. But only on the condition that he is in charge of this action."

I nod in agreement while waves of relief pass through me. "Thank you, gentlemen."

Alek inclines his head. "You know it's not going to be an easy mission, if we even get to do it."

"I know. I'm very thankful you've agreed to help me." I move my gaze to Witek. "Back in March, how did they know when and where the lorry with the prisoners were going to pass?"

"Well, Szkopy are good with their routines and punctuality. That's a huge advantage to us, but that's not enough." Witek runs his hand through his thick, brown hair and nods at Alek to continue.

Alek strides toward the window and sets aside a white curtain. "One of our boys works for a chocolate factory and distributes chocolate to Szucha every other day. He called and informed us when the lorry with the prisoners was going to pass."

"Can he help now too?" I ask, holding my breath.

"Not this time, he's currently out of Warsaw." Alek moves the curtain back and then lounges on the sofa next to Witek. "But there is this girl Kasia, who has made deliveries there a few times. She's new and hasn't helped us yet but she is willing to."

"She will call us with the time?" I ask as I feel adrenaline spike through my body.

"Yes, but only if she is able to find the information we need. No call means either she doesn't know or there's no transport that day."

"When is she scheduled to go there?"

"Tomorrow. If we get the call from her, we will take up positions on Długa Street, the most likely route the lorry will take on the way to Pawiak."

"We believe it's best to take the same approach as in March, and attack with gasoline bottles, submachine guns and grenades," Witek says. "You have the rest of today and tomorrow to plan the details and distribute weapons to the boys." He gets up. "Just know, I'm sure of retaliations if this mission succeeds."

I swallow hard at the thought of it, but I know there is no way back from this now.

TWENTY-FOUR

MATEUSZ

11 June 1943

The next day I can't focus until it's time to meet at Pan Józef's flat on Bonifaterska Street. By now things are planned and people know their assignments. Besides Alek and myself, there are another dozen boys from Kedyw waiting for Alek's instructions. Even though the place is packed, everyone seems quiet. Some whisper amongst themselves, others are busy cleaning their guns, but the air in the room brims with something close to nostalgia and awe.

This place has that sort of impact. Pan Józef passed last year at the advanced age of ninety-four. He worked with the resistance to the end, and urged Witek to keep using his flat. He was a national hero for us and everyone respected him.

When I was a young boy, my father sometimes took me to visit Pan Józef. I always listened with rapt attention to his stories, such as about the time he helped with the January Uprising in 1863 as a boy or fought in the war in 1914 for our independence. The fact that he knew Marshal Piłsudski, always impressed me in my young years. My father valued his wisdom and always said that thanks to people like him this nation survived 123 years of annexation. Thanks to people like him, those who held Poland in their hearts against all odds, our homeland came back on the maps again. He reminds us, even now, that Poland will never stop existing in the hearts of its people, and this will lead us to a long-awaited victory.

The flat seems to have a life of its own after Pan Józef's passing. The same shelves stuffed with old books, the same photographs showing special moments from his life, like the one when he met Piłsudski for the first time. The same antique sofa that served him for decades or an open book on the side table where he'd left it planning to come back to it. No one has touched it, as if expecting him to walk in any minute, tell us a story and continue reading his book.

I shake off my thoughts, to be ready when the time comes. We all know nothing will happen though, if Kasia doesn't make the one call I'm praying for.

At nearly four o'clock the phone finally rings and a hand of fear clutches at my heart. I leap forward and pick up the receiver, feeling everyone's eyes on me. The air is thick with tension.

"Yes," I say and close my eyes awaiting the anticipated words.

"Hello, Uncle Jerzy," a female's cheery voice says. "I'm calling to remind you about our visit today around five. Will you be home?"

I feel sudden relief as pent-up tension releases. These are the exact words Kasia was to say if she knew the transport would be happening today. I force my mind to focus on delivering the coded response. "Oh yes, darling, you can count on me being here."

When I'm done, I turn to Alek and nod, meeting his serious gaze. "She said in about an hour," I say.

"We need to get to our positions soon then." Alek's tone is

calm but a stern note of finality rings through it. There is no room for being afraid. He always reassures us that things will go well and everyone under his command is safe. It's why I have a tremendous trust in him. He is a true warrior.

People shuffle from their seats but he instructs us not to leave together. "In small groups, gentlemen."

Half an hour later everyone is ready at the right positions on Dluga Street which as always brims with crowds of people who rush with their tasks before curfew. Our boys all blend in. Witek ordered that I stay aside and let Alek and his crew do things their way. After all, they do have much more experience than me. I had no choice but to agree but I know I will do whatever is needed for this action to be successful.

I stay behind a cigarette kiosk, pretending to read wall announcements. Alek engages in conversation with a stranger in a black elegant suit, but his watchful eyes are in the right places. He keeps both hands in the pockets of his long, raven overcoat. His weapon is ready.

I'm sure that for any trespasser, things look the same as always, that's how well his boys sink into the crowd.

Now it's ten minutes to five. Alek's nervous gaze rests on Jacek, who stands at the corner with his rickshaw. The plan is that when he spots the lorry, he waves.

I swallow hard when a uniformed German officer approaches him and climbs into his bike's front cart.

Jacek's questioning gaze scoops to Alek who nods. I see the point. It's better that he drives away with the armed officer and someone else takes his place to signal about the lorry.

But just before Jacek pedals away, he looks back and rapidly waves like he just saw a good friend. The truck is approaching.

I swallow hard and touch the pistol in my pocket. God, please help us with this.

As the lorry nears, we realize that another German car

follows it. But there is no time for hesitation as the mission must be fulfilled.

A group of our boys leaps forward and tosses a set of petrol bombs into the front of the lorry. The sound of broken glass and squealing tires makes the crowd around me yell in panic. Everyone tries to run away or hide while a gush of fire overtakes the front of the car with prisoners.

The driver's head lands on the steering wheel while the other two uniformed Germans from the front surge behind the car and begin shooting. The German soldiers from the other vehicle do the same thing and the shooting soon escalates into a frantic exchange between them and our people.

Alek prompts his boys to move even closer and they manage to hit and kill the two of them, but the other ones are relentless and they have submachines.

Alek signals to throw grenades at the second car and that works well but it seems like there are more soldiers now shooting from behind the lorry.

Soon I realize this direct exchange between two sides won't lead us to victory. Our boys are aggressive with their attack and a few of them use submachine guns, but the exchange is taking way too long and it's going to attract more Germans from the neighborhood.

Alek surprises me by appearing beside me behind the kiosk from where I've been shooting as well. His breathing is labored but soon he catches his breath and says, "I have to try to cross the road and take them from the back. It's the only way." He points to his people who keep attacking. "It's taking way too long."

I nod. I should have thought of it, after all I'm more to the side of the entire shuffle. "I'll go with you," I say, for the first time realizing that I've no fear in me. I will do everything to help and the only thing I feel right now is adrenaline.

He shakes his head. "No, better stay here, just in case." He springs forward and crosses the cobbled road. I expect him to be struck by a bullet any time just like one of his people was before but he passes unnoticed by the Germans who are too busy exchanging fire with our boys.

He takes position closer behind the courtyard gate and begins shooting from there. He strikes one of them but the others realize his presence and shoot his way too.

Just after he hits another soldier, he suddenly goes quiet. Something is not right; I don't think he was hit.

Without another thought, I leap forward and cross the street but halt in the alley between the buildings, sensing something eerie is going on. Then I slide to the back of the building belonging to the courtyard Alek went into and lurk around the tenement to approach the gate from the rear.

There it is: a man dressed in a long black leather jacket pointing his pistol at him.

No, no, not right now when we are so close to winning this. I feel like I'm choking when I spot Alek's pistol tossed in front of the man.

His face is white and concentrated like he is ready to jump at the stranger. He must see me behind his captor but he shows no indication.

Something angry and powerful awakens within myself and I settle on a desperate resolution that just comes to my mind. Without another thought and ready to die, I leap forward and bump into the man's back. He turns his pistol my way and somehow manages to press the trigger.

I feel no pain, just a small pinch in my arm and I'm dazed. I still have enough strength to kick the gun from man's hand as he thumps down. Then, Alek smashes his fist into the man's face and keeps repeating until he is unconscious.

"Are you okay?" he says, running his gaze over me.

But happy shouts in the back distract us. Our boys must

have succeeded in taking the other German soldier down as right now crowds of prisoners run out from the lorry.

We spring forward and I can't help but yell, "We did it!" I bump into running prisoners hoping to spot Felek but he is nowhere. Maybe he isn't on this transport? We knew it was possible but from the very beginning I believed otherwise. Only when there are no more people, do I hop inside the truck and exhale with relief at the sight of Felek on the floor. His face is covered with blood and deep wounds, and his eyes are closed, so I shake him.

"Felek, it's me." No response, so I rattle his arms again and that's when he stirs.

"We need to hurry up," Alek roars behind me.

I reach to scoop Felek up but that's when I notice that my right arm is bleeding. For the first time I feel excruciating pain. How didn't I notice it earlier?

Alek grabs Felek and we run out toward the car our boys brought over.

TWENTY-FIVE

ANNA

Helmut's attitude changed significantly. Now he visits my café almost every day making sure that other men don't go as far as even glancing at me. He keeps introducing me to his work friends as his *beloved* wife causing my stomach to twist every time he does it. But I pretend because I know how dangerous he is.

It seems he's had more to drink tonight than usual because at midnight he still remains at his chair, sipping brandy and watching me. Everyone else has gone.

I yawn. "I'm tired. Hope you don't mind if I close my café?"

He grins. "Of course, darling. Lock the door and let's go upstairs."

The moment he says it, the strong need to punch him grows in me. I close my eyes and try to reason with him. "Please, Helmut, do not complicate things. You need to get some sleep too." I put pressure on my last words. "In your own home."

"It's absurd. You're rightfully my wife and I'm the only man entitled to sleep in your bed."

I bite my lip but adopt a calm tone of voice. "You know very well that this marriage is only on paper. You made your choice to love another woman a long time ago. You didn't want me from the beginning and you treated me horribly, so don't lie now either."

"You don't know me at all. In fact, you don't even try to get to know me. You've already judged me as a bad guy and you don't care to know why I'm the way I am."

His unexpected words stun me. Are there tears in his eyes? Why is he doing this? Why is he playing games with me? We both know he can force me to take him upstairs, and if I disagree, he can easily drag me to Szucha where I would be doomed. So why does he pretend to be in such pain instead? I don't believe a word he says. "I'm just tired. I've had a long day."

"Yes, I didn't want you because I loved someone else. I loved the woman that was forbidden to me, first by my own father who threatened to disinherit me if I married her, and then the war took her away. I tried protecting her despite it all, and in the end I have, though she can never be mine." He rises and kneels before me. "You are the one that rightfully deserves to stand by my side, and you must accept it. I just want you to know."

"Why are you telling me all of this?" I can't listen to this. It's all pretend. Obviously, he doesn't want to force me to go back to him. He wants to fool me into believing he's changed, but I know better.

"Because you must understand that I don't want to hurt you anymore."

"Then just leave me alone," I say, expecting his anger but there is no reaction.

His gaze is absent now as he stares into the air. "Through my years of growing up, my father often traveled abroad to take care of business while my sister and I stayed with Mutti on one of our estates. I'm five years senior to Inga, so she wasn't aware of things. But I was." He pauses and takes a deep breath, then exhales.

"Mutti was always beautiful and many men were attracted to her. Now she is an imitation of herself confined to her bedroom in her illnesses. Anyway, back then her beauty was noticeable and she liked to flirt with men when my father wasn't around. But one day I realized it didn't stop only at that, she cheated on my father with every male who ever worked on his estate. She cheated on him with everyone who showed her interest and I kept seeing those men in her bed or other places throughout the estate."

"Why are you telling me this?" I ask, holding on to the last threads of my patience.

He ignores my question and continues his tale, "One time when I was a teenager, I found the courage to ask her why she did it. She wasn't ashamed, instead she smiled and told me that my father isn't enough for her and that she feels lonely with him. I see her point now about that. My father is a cold man who cares about his fortune and nothing else. Anyway, it all stopped when one of her lovers blackmailed him. He threatened to reveal my mother's affairs to society if my father didn't pay him a vast amount. He paid him but also threw her damn lover out and he went to speak to my mother."

"Helmut, please. I don't need to know this as it doesn't change anything between us," I say but he carries on with his story anyway.

"I eavesdropped on the entire conversation. He basically told her that since divorce is not acceptable in his family, he would have to kill her if she didn't stop. It worked but since then she has given in to melancholia and anxiety, and plenty of medication. I'm telling you this, so you understand me more. My father was the one running both of our lives, forcing us into this marriage. The only mistake I made was punishing you for it. Now I want to make up for it. I want to prove to you that you can have a dignified life beside me. In return, I only expect you to comply. The world must see that we are a happy couple, and then I can climb the career ladder much easier."

So, this is all about his career. He told me his childhood story, so I'll feel bad for him and comply with his demands while he continues his murderous work at Szucha. What a disgusting and manipulative man, blaming his evil nature and his faults on his mother and father.

TWENTY-SIX

MATEUSZ

20 January 1944

"I thought you would like to know that," I say to Anna as we sip on a black ersatz coffee at her kitchen table. It's been awkward between us since our conversation the day she came over to comfort me after Mietek's death. She doesn't even know how much I wanted to make love to her that day. I was eaten by sadness after my friend died and at the same time confused about my scrambled feelings toward her. But I had enough decency in me not to take advantage of her, because going to bed with her would have been about comforting my broken soul. She deserves much more than that and I keep that in mind every time my heart skips at her touch.

"Yes, I do," she says and wipes a tear from her cheek. "It's important to me to know that my little Rutka is fine. I'm sure she is safer out in the country than here, even though she's still in hiding."

"I believe that too. Living in Warsaw is extremely dangerous right now, so she is better off over there."

She nods. "I wish I could tell her how much I miss her."

I want to kiss that soft smile. I know she was hurt when I blurted out about her being married. I still can't forgive myself for doing it. "One day you will, I'm sure of that."

She sighs. "One day. How's Felek doing?"

"He's definitely on his way to getting better. My old school friend has a small estate near Gdańsk where Felek is safe until he recovers. It's a miracle he survived."

"A miracle thanks to your determination," she says, playfully nudging my arm. "Witek told me all about it."

"If not for Alek and the boys from Kedyw none of this would be possible."

"Alek is good at operating under the hardest circumstances. Such an honorable young man. By the way, Witek said you were injured too?" She points to my other arm.

I shrug. "Just a scratch. Nothing worth mentioning."

"Modest as—" A rapid knock on the door interrupts her.

We listen for the familiar pattern but it's just a chaotic rumble.

"I've no idea who would be visiting so early," she says. "Please go wait in my bedroom in case it's one of the café guests."

I do as she asks, knowing I will be ready should she need me.

"Hello, my dear wife," a male's voice greets Anna. It's that piece of work—her Nazi husband, one of the biggest tyrants on Szucha who enjoys torturing even women. Felek recognized him and said the son of the bitch was one of his interrogators and beat him unconscious with his whip. I clench my fists. He's top of the list of the sleazebags to be eliminated by the resistance. If only we didn't face terrible retaliation... They're capable of killing so many Poles for one of theirs.

"What a surprise," Anna says in her well-played voice. "I was about to go out."

"It's the same thing you always say whenever I visit. You're only civil to me at the café when there are other people around. Why is that?" His tone is insistent but I also sense some violence in it.

"I don't know what you're talking about. If you will excuse me, please."

There is some shifting around for a moment making me touch my pistol. But soon his voice comes, "I'm tired of your games. I've been patient for so long while waiting for you to move into my villa, but you keep avoiding me. I won't stand for this anymore. You have a day to pack as I will send a car tomorrow for your belongings. I will take much more extreme measures should you disobey me, my dear wife."

"You know I have to be here for the café." Anna's voice is strained. He must be grabbing her. Just the thought of him touching her sends anger through me. My jaw hurts from my clenched teeth.

"And you still can by traveling here during the day but for the evening and night your place is at home, next to me where you belong. I can't stand the gossip anymore. Once and for all, we need to show everyone the respected married couple we are." After a short pause he continues, "Besides, I will not allow you to entertain men at night here any longer. I've heard a few stories from my friends in the office."

"You're going too far." Her stable voice makes me close my eyes. How I feel for her.

He utters a malicious laugh. "This is nothing. If you disobey me, I will prove to you what I'm capable of. You either live with me or in the prison. If I can't have my own wife, no one else will have her. I don't think I can be any clearer."

The door bangs and there is silence.

~

I can't focus for the rest of the day. He basically left Anna no choice. She has to move in with him or he will arrest her. We all know he doesn't even need a valid reason to do it, and he can just make something up. This man will stop at nothing to ruin her life. He will probably resume beating her the moment she moves in with him.

At my meeting with Witek in his flat, I tell him what happened today.

He wrinkles his forehead. "That's not good. He kept some distance until now. Something must have pushed him to force her into moving in with him. I wonder if he suspects anything."

"I don't think so. It seems he got angry that Anna brings men from the café for the night. He kept repeating that she belongs to him."

"So that's what it is." He sighs and runs his hand through his hair. "I've been talking to Zdzisiek about planning to eliminate him. But it will take time that Anna doesn't have anymore."

"What needs to be done and how long it will take?"

"First of all, we need approval from the chiefs, then research about his habits as you know very well it can't be done randomly. It has to be planned, because he is very careful. His work peers accompany him everywhere, even when he comes over to visit Anna."

"We can't let her move in with him." The vision of her sharing bed with him hits me with the force of a hammer. I would rather die than let that happen.

"You know Anna, she will be fine. She is good at playing games and she will do it for as long she needs to."

"At what cost?" My heart pounds while heat flushes through my body.

He avoids my gaze and takes out a cigarette. While inhaling, he closes his eyes as if trying to gather his thoughts. When he speaks, his voice is quiet. "What do you suggest?"

My breath bottles up in my chest. "I will take care of him."

"You?" His eyes measure me up.

"It has to be done when he leaves his house in the morning. He won't expect it and that's when most likely he will be alone."

"How do you imagine this? Jumping at him from the bush?"

I bang my fist on the table. "Stop mocking me, goddammit! You know it's the only way to save her."

"Don't raise your voice at me." His tone is calm but disciplinary. "Hold your horses before I lose my temper."

I sigh and bend my head. "I'm sorry."

He exhales loudly and leans back in his chair. "All right. I know that when you're determined about something, nothing can change your mind. And you are pretty much set on helping Anna. You know the risk you're about to take on?"

"I do. It's no time to plan an action. I will simply wait for him and shoot him."

"I can't believe I'm agreeing to this. You'll probably listen to your conscience at the last minute and spare him. That's how you are, Mateusz."

"No, not this time. He's the one who keeps ordering ghetto executions of our people. The quicker we get rid of him, the more lives will be saved."

"You forgot about one thing."

I shake my head. "If he stays alive, way more people will die. And you know it."

He absently tags at the vinyl tablecloth. "If this goes in accordance with your plan and you succeed, and assuming you escape, you will have to leave Warsaw for some time. You don't know who will witness it. There are eyes around. For the sake of your family, and ours, you will join partisans outside the city. No one can know your whereabouts. That's the only condition on which I will agree to this."

TWENTY-SEVEN

ANNA

Another sleepless night. I smoke cigarette after cigarette while suppressing my tears. It's my end. Standing up to Helmut will do no good. He will go after me and the café. The only sensible thing is to move in with him but just the thought of it makes me sick to my stomach. I have to pack by the end of the day and be ready for him. Every piece of me is paralyzed by his presence in my life again. Except now, he is a ruthless tormentor believing blindly in the Nazis' sickness.

With a heavy heart, I prepare for the move, telling myself it's only for a short time. I will make sure to spend whole days running my café, so what terrifies me the most are the nights in the same house with him. The thought of those nights alone with him make me want to cry. I feel like the lost girl back in Germany, lying in my bed and praying that he would not show up. But most times, he barged into my bedroom to use my body for his primitive needs. Afterwards, I always cried myself to sleep.

The memory of the loneliness and hurt washes over me anew. I must remember that terrified girl doesn't exist anymore.

She was replaced long time ago by the headstrong and sophisticated woman who makes sure to keep an emotional distance from people. The only time I failed was with Mateusz. I was ready to give him my heart like that naïve girl back then. But he rejected me because of my *marriage*. What irony—something I thought I left behind for good had chased away the only man I felt for, and now I have to live with this devil again.

To my astonishment, Helmut's car never shows up. Maybe he was just trying to intimidate me and prove that things are done on his terms and I'm at his mercy. Or perhaps it's a test to see if I show up at his door anyway. How I hate him. I wish him the worst. I wish him dead.

~

In the morning, I go about my tasks as usual and work on the supply list for the café when someone knocks at the door. I quickly realize it's not the pattern used by the resistance, so with my heart in my throat, I slide forward to listen.

"Frau Liberchen, please open the door," a man's arrogant-like voice barks in German.

A cold tremor runs through my body. It must be Gestapo. Did Helmut send them to arrest me because I didn't show up at his door last night? He wastes no time.

The knock doesn't stop for the next few minutes. "Frau von Liberchen, we know you're home. Please open up."

Maybe it's not the Gestapo after all. They would definitely have broken in by now. I clear my throat and say, "Who is there?"

"We have extremely important information for you, please open the door, or we will take our own measures." The voice is threatening now. So, it is Gestapo.

I turn the key with my trembling hands and gesticulate to two men in long leather jackets to come in."

Without hesitation, they stride toward the kitchen and take seats at my table while I follow them, unsure what to do.

"Please have a seat with us, Frau. We've a few questions," a tall man with a scar across his cheek says, his teeth grinding in an eerie smile.

I don't get easily intimidated by other people but something about this man makes my muscles twitch.

I swallow the lump in my throat and say, "Would you like something to drink, gentlemen?"

"Please don't bother yourself, Frau von Liberchen," a dark-haired man with a mustache says. He scrutinizes me but there is something about him that makes my inner alarm not tingle so much. "Please forgive our intrusion but we came on a rather important matter."

I nod and take my seat across from them. What do they want? If they were here to arrest me, they would have already done it. I sense it's something else.

"Where were you yesterday morning around seven?" the man with the scar asks while eyeballing me.

I'm relieved I can tell them the truth. "I was home, still in my bed. This weather makes me very lethargic in the morning and with the café's long hours, I allow myself extra sleep."

He nods. "When was the last time you saw your husband?"

"The day before yesterday. He paid me a visit." Why would they ask these questions? Wouldn't Helmut tell them that? Is he in trouble? My hopes soar.

"So, you don't live together?" the same man asks.

I'm not sure how much they know and how open Helmut has been about our marriage. What's safe to say? "No, not since Helmut moved to Warsaw but," I spread my hands and gesture toward the rest of the flat, "as you see I've packed as we decided I move into his villa and travel here to manage my café."

"Yes, we noticed your trunks," the dark-haired man says. "So, you were going to move in with your husband when?"

"He was supposed to send the car yesterday but he must have forgotten. I'm sure I will hear from him today though. He is probably very busy, just like you gentlemen." I smile, making sure it reaches my eyes.

TWENTY-EIGHT

MATEUSZ

One day earlier

For any other mission, we prepare in advance, but this time it's different. I don't even have a detailed plan. I don't know what time in the morning he leaves the house and if he's going to be alone. Is there anyone else living in the villa with him? There are a lot of huge question marks, but I'm certain of one thing: I must kill him, so the lives of others can be spared and Anna doesn't have to suffer anymore because of him. He is the scoundrel who ordered so many executions of Poles in the ruins of the ghetto. He is known for taking sick pleasure in torturing others.

I feel like an amateur without a stable plan, but I know what I'm here for and I won't leave until I do what I can to accomplish it. One thing is for sure: one of us will be dead today.

I reach his villa near seven o'clock in the morning. Everything appears gloomy and hazy, and once more I curse myself for forgetting my gloves. I keep my hands in my coat's pocket, where my pistol rests. I pass the two-story villa a few times while checking the surroundings. It's the quieter part of

Warsaw, so I encounter no patrol at that time of the day. The curfew is still in force, so I've no passersby to worry about. Plus, even dogs wouldn't risk going out this early into such low temperatures.

I decide to change the plan and act as his visitor, even though it's so early in the morning. The iron gate makes a squeaky noise when I open it. It's a very risky thing to appear at his door since neighbors could see me through the window but I've no choice. Once I'm on the other side of the fence, I move to the entrance of the house trying to make as little noise as possible but the snow on the ground doesn't work in my favor and it's impossible to avoid the crunchy little sounds of my footsteps.

Everything around me is still iced besides a few chirping birds, so I exhale with relief. There is a high chance that no one saw me. He might be still sleeping, or someone else might open the door. I don't even know if he came back home for the night.

I wipe sweat from my forehead and wait for my heart to slow down. For a moment, I forgot the winter's harshness but soon enough it's snowing again and I curse myself once more for not taking those damn gloves.

It would have been wiser to spend at least a few days watching him to learn his habits and surroundings and then pick the right moment to hit and run. But I could not stand one more day with the knowledge that the bastard could hurt Anna whenever he felt like.

Nothing can stop me from going ahead with my plan. I knock at the door and wait a couple of minutes. No commotion on the other side, so I tap the door with more force this time.

Soon enough someone comes to the door and grumbles in a sleepy voice through a peephole, "Who the hell is that?"

It must be him and it seems as if he just awoke which makes him perhaps more vulnerable.

I make all the effort to sound in impeccable German. "Your

wife asked me to deliver some of her trunks, sir. She's also sending a personal note."

He still doesn't open the door but his voice is suspicious now. "This early?"

"Yes, sir. Frau instructed me yesterday to make the delivery as early as possible. She gave me no more details. Should I come back at a later time?"

"I told her I would send the car but the woman is just so impulsive." He laughs. "Which surprises me greatly. Fine—"

The moment he pushes the door open, I force my sweaty hand out of the pocket and press the trigger aiming at his heart. I take no moment to think but the way his eyes widen in terror is not lost on me.

While he slips to the floor, my instincts shout at me to turn and run, but some other invisible power makes me kneel beside him and make sure one bullet did its job.

His pale blue eyes are still open but now seem absent. He mumbles, "Forgive me, Ruth. My love." Then he is gone.

As adrenaline shoots through my entire system, I spring to my feet and run, worrying it's too late and someone heard the gunshot. But I'm able to escape without encountering anyone, then I slip through the still quiet streets of my hurting city. My heart hammering, my soul broken. I just killed another human.

When I get to my flat, there is only one picture in my mind now: those last flickers of pure terror in his eyes when he realized what was happening. His soft whisper asking for forgiveness from another woman. Not Anna, but Ruth. Who was that woman that came to his mind in his last breaths? The truth is that I didn't expect this kind of reaction from him. It was as if he accepted his sentence in the blink of an eye, and then was afraid like any other human would. Because of that, he left this mark on my soul and it hurts to no extent. I killed another man. That was the naked truth.

It's different killing someone during a fight from a far

distance, but it was another thing to do it while looking someone in the eyes. To face someone so closely while killing him, was a heart-wrenching experience for me. It was a silent shock. I know it will stay with me for the rest of my life like a stain on my conscience.

In the end, I know I did the right thing. I killed the man who ordered the deaths of so many, and I freed Anna from her tormentor. Now it was time to pack and disappear for the sake of my family.

TWENTY-NINE

ANNA

The dark-haired Gestapo man clears his throat and says, "Unfortunately, Frau von Liberchen, your husband will not show up today or any other day."

I go completely still. Did Helmut get in trouble and the Gestapo is going after me now? "I don't understand."

"He was shot dead at his villa yesterday morning by a Polish criminal," the man with the scar says while carefully watching my reaction.

Instinctively, I cover my face with my hands and sob like I've found out terrible news about someone I truly loved. "No, no, no," I keep slurring the words out. "That's impossible."

"Please accept our deepest condolences," the dark-haired man says while clapping my back. "Your husband was a great, honorable man and he will be missed by so many. Rest assured, we will be seeking revenge for his death. It's a tremendous loss to the entire Gestapo."

I cry even harder now, just like I did during one of my plays in the theatre.

"We will respect your privacy now but please don't hesitate to contact us should you need any assistance."

I nod. "Thank you. I will."

The man with the scar stands up too and adds, "We will be back soon as we have more questions to ask."

When they are gone, I want to dance and yelp in happiness. I can't believe Helmut is dead. I'm truly a free woman. The man who terrified me so much cannot harm me anymore. My hate toward him doesn't allow me to feel sorry for him. He got what he deserved and he won't hurt anyone else again. This war has changed me so much and I have no compassion for the enemy at all. At the same time, it scares me to know how cold-hearted I've become. Well, there was not a single good memory that I cherished with Helmut. Only pain and humiliation, and now I don't have to worry about him.

I know who is behind this—Mateusz killed him. I saw the hard determination in his eyes that day after Helmut left my apartment. Mateusz didn't say much to me but said he had something urgent to take care of. I was so hurt by his indifference to Helmut's threats, but now I understand what he meant.

The war has changed him too. It's pushed him beyond all boundaries, ones he never expected to cross. I never thought he would do this, though. I didn't expect he would be capable of killing someone in cold blood without caring for the consequences. Surely someone saw him. But that's the thing about Mateusz—he is a gentle soul with plenty of compassion for others, but when something gets into him, he doesn't relent. His actions might not be planned well and he relies on a spontaneous act, but he doesn't stop when he believes in the purpose of something. I can't even imagine how much it cost him to do what he did. I yearn to hug him and most of all, to thank him.

Days go by, then weeks. The Gestapo men show up a couple more times and ask many questions. They tell me that the Polish resistance did it and they assure me that they even suspect a certain man. They've issued letters after him.

I know I need to warn Mateusz but he has disappeared and

Witek keeps telling me that he has no idea where he could be. No one knows. I suspect he decided to stay away from Warsaw for a while, just to be on the safe side.

I tell my worries to Witek but he refuses to believe that Mateusz was the one who killed Helmut. He says that it makes no sense. I don't agree with him. I know it was him and I just hope he isn't in trouble because of that. I tried to find out his whereabouts but no one knows anything. Not even Zdzisiek or Alek Zatopolski, no one knows.

Poor Wanda keeps reading announcements with the red lists of people sentenced to death, just to make sure that Mateusz is not one of them. I don't know where she finds the strength to do it. At least we have each other. That makes it easier to keep the hope going that he is still alive.

PART 2

THE UPRISING & AFTER THE WAR

*"I know from my own experience
that being a strong woman
brings a lot of loneliness.
Everyone around you assumes you are self-sufficient
and can hold onto every load that life throws at you.
But like everyone else,
even the strongest woman needs warmth and compassion."*
~Anna Otenhoff

THIRTY

MATEUSZ

14 August 1944

The uprising started on the first day of August and that's when I joined it, after a long trip from Tosaki. I found my place in one of the squads fighting in Wola, a district in western Warsaw.

Several parts of the city were held by our units within the first days, and Wola was no exception. Even when Germans began their major attacks on the fifth day, we still managed to halt them with heavy fire.

But that's when the tragedy began in the parts of Wola which stayed under the Germans. Their troops went from house to house to shoot everyone, even the elderly, women and children. Everyone. Rape. Murder. Torture. They burned down hospitals with patients inside while others were killed in gunfire or mass executions. There was no mercy. The devil had his dance.

Their cruelty didn't stop at that. Once the German troops were strengthened with tanks on the seventh day, they forced civilian women and children onto the tanks as human shields when attacking us. Thanks to this barbaric move, within two days they'd made significant advances and cut the Wola district in half. Their other bestial way was to form the innocent civilians into line and use them as barricade when they shot at us. How could we shoot back? Just at the thought of it I experience body tremors.

By the eleventh day, our last unit was forced to leave Wola and retreat to Stawki Street. It was my squad. We fought for the next two days over the Stawki but we stood no chance against their armature and backed down to the Old Town. By losing Stawki we let Germans encircle us in The Old Town without any way out. Now they will intensify their attack on here.

I have a few hours to rest before going back to the front line, so I'm reclining on the armchair in the flat assigned as my unit's base. Everyone in this dim room is in slumber after long days of exhaustion. Everyone beside me. My bothersome thoughts don't allow for any shuteye despite my tiredness. Faces of innocent people flood my brain and send shivers down my spine. I will never be the same man, not after what I witnessed in Wola, not after second-hand accounts I heard.

Feeling sudden claustrophobia, I slip from the room and walk down the stairs into an empty courtyard. I breathe in a gush of air as relief washes over me. I thought I was going to suffocate up there when I couldn't catch a breath. I find a bench made of wood board, and supported by bricks. In the far distance, artillery sounds almost never stop. They are getting closer and closer.

"I was looking for you." Witek's quiet voice brings me back to reality. I saw him earlier in the day when the base was assigned to us. My old friend claps my back and settles beside me. "You boys did a good job."

I shrug. "So what if we ended up here and couldn't help all these innocent people who were slaughtered." I don't care to leave out all the pain from my voice. How else I can talk about it? Pretend nothing happened and move to the next stage of the fight? Yet I know that in order to not go insane, it's exactly what I need to do—step up into the next battlefield without over-thinking.

"I heard what was happening there." His voice holds layers of tremors that causes pain in my heart. "But that's what those murderers want. They committed those terrible atrocities in Wola to crush our will to fight and bring the uprising to a quick end. But they don't realize that after what they did to our people over there, our resistance only strengthened. They will pay for what they did. Remember my words."

"I hope so, my friend, I truly hope so."

"Listen, I have something important to talk to you about. We need fighters like you, but we also need your medical skills more now than ever." He gives me a meaningful look, making me wonder where he is going with this. He cannot possibly expect me to go back to being a doctor again.

"I'm a different person now. But it doesn't matter because the old world doesn't exist anymore."

"We're short on doctors. I had to order the set-up of another field hospital near here, because of how many wounded we have. I sent Anna over there a couple of days ago to supervise the place. Right now, we have a couple of nurses and decent equipment but we still need a doctor there."

"Anna is here?" I ask, feeling warmth at the mere thought of her.

He nods. "Yes, she is. Now I need you too, so more of our boys have a chance to survive."

"My responsibility is to fight."

"I know that but your skills are gold right now and by refusing to use them in aiding your brothers, you are failing your true responsibility."

"You were always good with words."

He answers with a soft laugh. "I'm a lawyer, after all. That's *my* greatest skill."

"I need to talk to my commander first," I say and close my eyes. How wonderful it would be seeing Anna again. Then guilt runs through me. It's not the time for such thoughts.

"I already spoke to him. Time is of the essence. They need you there immediately."

"Yes, chief," I say. "Do you happen to have any information on my sister?"

He sighs. "She was separated from Anna right at the beginning of the uprising. She was sent to work as a nurse in one of the hospitals, but Anna doesn't know which one. I did try locating her but had no luck." He puts his hand on my shoulder. "I've a strong feeling she is fine."

"Thank you, my friend. If you ever learn her whereabouts, please let me know. I pray every day for her safety."

"Of course." He gets up and walks a few steps away from me. "Try getting some sleep. I will come and get you in the morning."

THIRTY-ONE

ANNA

If not for the sisters from the nearby convent, I don't know how I would manage getting enough food for the hospital. I have great respect for these heroic women. They keep moving on and performing their everyday tasks like there are no bombs hitting buildings all around us. Thanks to their vegetable gardens, our patients have warm soup every day. They prepare bullions even from flowers like nasturtium.

Every time I stop over to help prepare the food, I find them sewing jackets out of blankets for our soldiers. They busy themselves with patching clothes and shoes for the insurgents, or even washing those men's linens. Their savviness keeps us fed and their beautiful hearts shine in this gloomy world.

Their convent is one of the few tenements in the Old Town that are still untouched. Sister Dorota told me once that God's hand keeps protecting them, so they can serve others and help our insurgents. I only asked her to pray for all of us here because our situation is grim right now with the Germans arriving any moment.

It's clear these wonderful sisters find strength in their faith, something I could never understand in the past. Now, though, seeing them being so selfless, I feel nothing but respect. I know from my own experience that being a strong woman brings a lot of loneliness. Everyone around you assumes you are self-sufficient and can bear every load that life throws at you. But like everyone else, even the strongest woman needs warmth and compassion. The sweet memory of my mother and thoughts of Mateusz being alive give me all of that despite the awful reality we live in. For those sisters, their faith in God is their backbone and the source of love.

THIRTY-TWO

MATEUSZ

The next morning, when Witek halts in front of ruins of a bombarded tenement, I give him a doubtful stare. "Are you certain this is the correct place?"

"Yes, I'm certain." As if reading my mind, he continues, "The field hospital is set in the basement. It's the safest place it can be in current situation." He sighs. "Especially now when Germans will intensify their attack on the Old Town."

I nod, knowing he is right. The building is already down, so the air bombers will not aim for it. But I can only imagine the harsh conditions down there.

We find a hole in the cellar beneath the ruins and go down into the field hospital. I wince at the familiar blend of lysine and fresh blood. The large room filled with iron beds is lit by kerosine lamps, and to my relief, there are a couple of tiny cellar windows. The hospital is buzzing with moans and conversations and it seems the thick air bothers no one.

I spot her right away. She leans by a bedridden man, holding a flask to his lips. Her blonde hair is under a white head covering and there is no hint of makeup on her face. Yet, her raw beauty takes my breath away. To be truthful, I didn't expect to feel such strong emotions at the mere sight of her.

She nods at something the man whispers to her, but then she lifts her gaze, meeting mine. I catch a glimpse of initial happiness flickering in her face.

The moment she smiles at me I know that I'm staring into the eyes of the woman I love more than life. This very realization hits me like a lightning bolt as cascade of strong emotions circulates through me. My heart bounds with pleasure and I wonder at the intensity of my feelings for her.

I completely forget my manners and stand like a fool gaping at her, still unable to shake the overpowering temptation to run and take her in my embrace.

But Witek steps forward. "Anna, dear, I have a doctor for you," he says and grins.

She moves her gaze from mine and walks toward us. "Hello, Mateusz," she says but doesn't smile at me anymore.

"Hello, Anna. Long time no see." I reach for her hand and bring it to my lips.

"I have no more time to spare, so I will leave you in Anna's hands. Any questions, ask her," Witek says and pats at my arm. "Thank you for agreeing to help us."

There is no time for a casual conversation as the moment Witek leaves new patients arrive. Anna quickly gives me a tour of the place. There is another small room with a table that will be used for surgeries and I note that there are instruments needed for basic procedures. She introduces me to two nurses, young girls who greet me with friendliness.

We work days and nights, taking turns for short breaks to sleep. The whole time Anna keeps her distance, and I wonder at it. First, I thought it was the amount of work, but soon I realize there is more to this. She holds a grudge toward me.

THIRTY-THREE

ANNA

Seeing Mateusz brought such happiness to me. I felt that fate finally decided to smile at me and give me this scrap of hope in the darkest of times. My initial desire was to run into his embrace and stay in it for a very long time. But then I reminded myself that I can't be even sure of his true feelings toward me. After all, he rejected me back then, when I went to talk to him after Mietek was killed. His harsh words reminding me of the fact I was married still pain me.

At the time when he said it, it hurt so much because he was the one person I thought understood me well. He knew what a bastard my husband was and that I had to run away from him to build a normal, dignified life.

Sometimes Mateusz was an enigma to me. There were moments when I was sure of his feelings, and then others when I doubted it. But I know he was the one who killed Helmut, so I could stay safe. Even though we weren't involved romantically, we definitely were friends.

The mission in Kraków changed a lot between us. That one dance in Wawel Castle especially opened my eyes to how tender he was toward me. He expressed his feelings in the sensual way he looked at me, and touched me. He made me feel like a princess. We danced surrounded by all sorts of Nazi criminals, yet I felt that this was the ball of my life because of the way he made me feel.

My illusion was crushed by his words when we were back in Warsaw. He made it clear that he didn't need me and whatever happened in Kraków wasn't as important as I thought.

I don't want to make the same mistake now. He's been respectful and visibly touched at seeing me again. But that's how Mateusz is in general—kind to everyone around him. I often hear nurses whispering between themselves that the handsome doctor is so nice and polite to them. The truth is that Mateusz Odwaga has a gentle soul, not made for this awful world. But when the war demanded him to kill another human being, he closed his eyes and let it guide him to fulfill his duties. He found the needed strength to do something he was so against. People like him are unique and should be cherished.

I keep my distance because I will never again make myself vulnerable to him or any other man. I'm aware of my feelings for him and I don't fight it anymore. These are mine and no one can take them away from me. Only my dear Wanda knows about it. It's a wonderful thing loving someone in such a pure, unconditional way. It makes you a better person even though it's just one-sided sentiment.

I'm proud of how brilliantly he manages working as the hospital's doctor. He pours his whole heart into it and offers the best care he can give to our patients.

I toss away my thoughts and walk to another tiny room with our dying patients. There is nothing we can do for them due to their fatal injuries. The only thing I can do is be there for them after I make sure the hospital has enough food and water, and when Mateusz or the nurses do not need my assistance. I'm not the most skilled but to help these men requires only a drop of humanity.

My tasks in this room are simple and consist of holding dying men's hands or holding a flask with water to their parched lips when they cry of thirst. Most of the time, they are unable to have any food due to their critical condition.

I'm not surprised when I find in there a young courier named Julia. She comes here every day during her sleep breaks and I get a strong sense from her that she wants to be left alone. She doesn't talk to anyone beside the dying men.

I let her be because the pain I see in her eyes breaks my heart. She went through some sort of trauma that keeps haunting her and is still unable to talk about it. So, we do not chat even when we spend hours here together.

I understand her. When Mutti died, it took months before I was able to go back to socializing with other people. That's how much it hurt. But I lived in a peaceful world that allowed me time to grieve. Julia doesn't have that. If she dwells too long in this pain, she may lose her life to it. She must wake up very soon from this state she is in if she wants to survive.

I will keep an eye on her and when it's time to push her forward, I will do it for her sake. She is so young and her whole life is ahead of her. Of course, if she is lucky enough to survive. For now, I just watch while she takes the needed time to grieve.

THIRTY-FOUR

MATEUSZ

One night, I get a chance for a brief rest, so I wander outside, planning to find a quiet spot within the ruins. I appreciate getting away from the stagnant air of the underground hospital even though up here I'm greeted by the waft of dust and burning. We had even more patients today due to one of the buildings collapsing after a bombing.

At first there was a submachine rattle in the distance but now it seems like both sides have decided to take a break as it's a silent night.

I lurch through the darkness but then freeze at the sight of Anna in the moonlight. She is feeding breadcrumbs to three pigeons.

I step forward and take a seat beside her against the single wall that still remains up. "It's not the best place to be right now," I say, watching the hungry birds fighting over the crumbs.

"It seems quiet today," she says without looking at me.

"I know. It's why I took my break now. I have a feeling it will get busy again later."

"I will go check on things down there," she says and attempts to rise but I hold her arm.

"Stay with me. I missed you." She's been avoiding me since the day she introduced me to the nurses and gave me a tour around the hospital.

She turns my way, her eyes blazing. "How dare you tell me that you missed me when you didn't even care to get in touch through all that time. Poor Wanda kept walking around the city just to check for your name on those awful red lists."

"I did it for your safety. After I killed..." I find it difficult to tell her that I killed her husband even though he was the cruelest son of a bitch.

"After you killed Helmut," she says in a quiet voice. "I knew it was you freeing me from this devil even though Witek never confirmed it."

"I agreed with Witek that disappearing for a while was a good plan." I close my eyes to suppress the pain and swallow hard. "But it didn't help at all. Maybe if my father knew my whereabouts, he would still be here now."

She places her hand on mine. "You know your father would never have told them even if he knew."

"You're right but it still hurts like hell knowing what happened to him."

She leans closer and our legs touch sending tingles of warmth through me. Her intense gaze meets mine. "You can't blame yourself for this. There will be a day when your pain changes into a sacred memory of your father. He will remain in your heart forever. I'm not saying it will ever stop hurting, but it will be a different type of pain."

Unable to keep my distance any longer, I pull her into my embrace. Our eye contact is so strong that I forget to blink. "Thank you for understanding me." Having her so close soothes all aches. "There was no day I didn't think or dream of you. That night when you came to talk to me after Mietek's death, I wasn't myself. I wanted to make love to you so badly but I had enough decency to know you deserved much more. Not a man that needed pity." I take a deep, savoring breath. "The truth is that I love you more than life." I caress her cheek with my thumb. I have to tell her my feelings. Life has proved over and over how fragile it can be. Before I kept convincing myself that I wasn't worthy of her but now I will do what my heart dictates.

Her smile is gentle like summer zephyr, her eyes are the ocean-blue of the sunniest day. "I love you," she whispers.

Her words have an immediate effect on my entire resolve. I crush my mouth to hers and we engage in a hungry kiss that unleashes all the pent-up emotions within myself. It's like I've waited for this very moment my entire life because never before have I felt such fulfillment.

The urgency of our kissing hastens my pulse and causes my heart to hammer in my chest. A moment later, I lift my mouth and whisper, "You're my heart."

THIRTY-FIVE

ANNA

He loves me. I didn't expect him to be so forward and honest with his feelings. The war truly changes people. It's as if he is afraid our time is running out and wants to cherish every moment we may still have. Death could claim us any day, just like it already has others.

I scamper through ruins and under barricades trying to pay less attention to rattling tanks, whistling bombs or the constant rumble in the air. The entire Old Town is in flames and I have no heart to contemplate the destruction. The Royal Castle and other heirlooms so bravely protected by Poles for centuries turned into cinders.

So many civilians are still hiding in the cellars of this bleeding Old Town with hope of survival but do they even have a chance? If these people can't escape to other parts of the city, most likely they will all die when Hitler's squads enter. How long can the Polish warriors withstand the powerful machinery of the evil?

The convent is only three blocks from the hospital, but because of the exchange of constant fire between both sides, it takes me over half an hour to get there.

I find the elderly sister Dorota in the garden where she hunches down, picking the weeds out. "Hello, sister Dorota. I came to see if I can be of any help in preparing today's broth."

She straightens up and wipes sweat from her forehead. "Oh, it's you, my dear child." Her wrinkled face crinkles with a bright smile. "Sister Malwina has it all under control. Why don't you take a seat with me?" She motions to a rusty bench under a birch tree. "My old bones call for a break."

We rest in the blissful shade and stay silent for a while, listening to artillery salvo in the distance. I like these natural ways of Sister Dorota when she doesn't force conversations.

She takes my hand in hers. "I've been noticing lately some light in your eyes despite the war. Are you in love, my child?"

Her words don't surprise me as she is a clever woman. Every time I come here, I enjoy talking to her. "Yes, sister. I can't stop my heart from feeling."

"It must be that doctor who can't take his eyes off you. God bless both of you and I pray he grants you survival and future happiness."

"Thank you for your kind words. But you see, I'm not sure if God will listen."

She wrinkles her forehead. "Why would you say that, my child? You must have hope."

I can't stop my nervous laugh. "Don't you see, sister, what is happening around us? I'm sorry to say it but God is not the one ruling right now. And it doesn't seem like he is doing anything to stop the evil."

An instant cloud of sadness comes to her amber eyes. "You're wrong, my child. God is merciful, and in the end, He will win over any evil."

"Please don't take me the wrong way. I know God exists and your kindness and sacrifice is pure proof of it. What you and other sisters do for us is a miracle. I just can't help but wonder why he doesn't stop all of this atrocity if he is so merciful? Why does he allow all this pain and injustice to innocent people? I can't even grasp it. You see, I grew up with a father who was a devoted atheist but my mother believed in God. When Papa wasn't at home, I often found her praying and she taught me basic prayers as well. I can still hear her voice telling me to always put my fate in God's hands. But later, life proved over and over that I must take my fate into my own hands or I won't survive. Now we live in times when I can't even do that. Everything is out of control and I feel so hopeless."

She doesn't answer right away but when she does, her voice is so calm and strong. "There are so many that wonder the very same thing you do. Some lost their faith because of it. But, my dear child, you must remember that God gave humans free will to decide. Whatever bad we witness on this earth comes from humans, not from God. And it's because they rejected His commandments. They took upon themselves to create this world the way they desire, not caring for their brothers and sisters. Jesus gave his life on the cross for our sins and it's up to us to live in faith. In the end, we all will be judged before Him, but here on earth, we are in charge of what we represent. People who choose evil cause others to suffer. But others like you, spread light and this is why the good will ultimately win."

"One brother is doing this to another," I whisper. I can't disagree with her about the fact that we humans decide our deeds. "It's just so impossible to understand where all this hate comes from."

"If people chose God, we would not have to worry about wars."

Sister Dorota's words stay with me for a long time. Her simple explanation was to the point, but still, I'm not sure what to think of it. There is so much misery and death around us right now that my world is shaken to the core. Yet I do what I can to help the ones that suffer, and there are many others like myself. We prove that there is still good in this world. If only I didn't have this empty feeling of hopelessness and uncertainty. One doesn't know when one's turn to die will come.

Lately, I've been thinking that the love I share with Mateusz is a twinkle of miracle that has no right to exist. At the same time, I wonder if love is not the most powerful weapon against all the hate.

THIRTY-SIX

MATEUSZ

29 August 1944

Days go by fast with more and more wounded men and women going through our underground hospital. Some injuries can be mended, some are terminal. It's the hardest part when the only thing we can do for these young people is hold their hand and be there for them so they don't die alone. We live on the run with less and less sleep as the Old Town succumbs more and more to German aggression, claiming several victims by each minute.

But even the damn war cannot change the strong feelings in me that shape the new meaning of my life. Loving Anna is like touching stars. What keeps us going through the darkest days are the stolen kisses, longing glances and rushed smiles. Just the thought that she is right there with me is enough to give me inner peace.

Since the nineteenth day of August, the Germans have significantly increased their invasion on the Old Town. It's obvious that their attacking squads are receiving tremendous support in the air and artillery from Luftwaffe and Wehrmacht.

The truth is we stand no chance against their constant assaults with our limited armory while being extremely outnumbered. So far the Soviets haven't rushed to aid us. It seems as if they're waiting for the Germans to kill us all before making their next move. Traitors.

Our days are filled with rumbles of incoming bombers and whistle of missiles that ignite buildings in flames killing innocent civilians who hide in cellars. There are no safe places for anyone anymore.

Entire streets turn into ruins and rubbish. Our historical treasures and relics that survived for centuries, are now demolished: castle, cathedral, gothic church, the old square buildings built five hundred years ago, Krasinski Palace, and many more. Everything turned into ruins.

We deal with a constant shortage of bread and water, any kind of food. On the fourteenth day of August, Germans turned off the water supply in the entire city, and now most of the wells that our people managed to build have been destroyed. But Anna keeps finding ways to make sure our patients have at least one meal a day and enough to drink. I don't know how she does it, but she does, and I'm afraid to ask in case I jinx it.

This morning I managed to save a young man's leg from amputation but the surgery took a long time. The leg is all stitched now and the nurses just moved him to one of the spare beds in the main room. I clean my hands and wipe sweat from my forehead. I feel like I'm about to collapse from more than twenty-four hours on constant duty. Time to get at least a few hours of sleep, so I'm able to continue this ordeal.

Then I see her standing in the door, staring at me with a terrified look in her eyes. "What is it?" I ask. The first thing that comes to my mind is that we're completely surrounded and the Germans are here.

"Witek was killed." Her broken voice slices waves of aches through my heart.

I swallow a painful lump. "It can't be," I whisper, locking my gaze with hers. But all I find there are sorrow and desperation. "When? How?" A sudden lock of energy sweeps through my body as I try to grasp cruel reality.

She sniffs and wipes at her nose. "Yesterday. He was crossing the barricade and that's when the German sniper—"

I pull her into my embrace and we cry together. No more words—only tears for our dear friend and chief.

Soon though we are called to our duties. The dull pain stays in me while I busy myself taking care of injured men. Anna's words replay in my mind over and over but I still deny them. It seems as if Witek will appear anytime to check on us. I refuse to accept the truth because I know it would break me.

At the same time, being able to cry while feeling Anna's touch, makes it easier. She loved and respected him the same way I did and she understands my pain. We've lost the man who from the very first day of the war refused to give up. He had the resistance in him from the beginning and we all felt it and took strength from it. He was our guide in the most difficult times, our conscience when it came to any tough decision, our stamina in the middle of hell, our hope for the future.

It's damn hard to move on with life but I have no choice. There are too many people right now that need me. Way too many.

"Doctor Odwaga, they brought a new patient that is unconscious and covered in blood," Hania, a raven-haired nurse says.

Without a word, I follow her to the main room and busy myself checking the man. I find no visible wounds and his breathing is normal. I recognize him right away. It's Leszek, the lowlife that almost got Anna and myself killed. My doctor ethics tell me to help him despite it all. I don't hate him; I just feel pity for him. I know hating him would make me a miserable man. But I do have a strong urge to throw him out of here.

"He is covered in someone else's blood," I say to Hania.

"Let's leave him to awake on his own." I step away but add before leaving, "He needs a good wash."

I forget about Leszek until the same nurse approaches me hours later. "Doctor Odwaga, the patient that was covered in someone else's blood is awake now. I gave him some water and he ate a bowl of broth. I thought maybe you'd want to take a look at him."

I whisper a prayer for the ability to control myself. When I near him, Leszek is busy flirting with a pretty and young nurse whose name is Magda. She clearly avoids him, feeding another man whose hands are covered by bandages.

"What is such a beauty like yourself doing in this dungeon?" Leszek says and grabs at her bottom.

She moves his hand away and says, "Please behave, or I will call the doctor."

"I see you're doing well, Leszek," I say. It takes a lot of my inner discipline not to throw him out the bed. "Let me do some examining here."

At first, his mouth falls open but he recovers in no time and glares at me. "What are you doing here, Odwaga? I should have known that a pathetic coward like you would do everything to avoid fighting."

I ignore his insult and grab my stethoscope to check his heartbeat but he shouts at me, "Do not touch me, you bastard."

I won't let him provoke me. These people are going through so much and they don't need to witness this. "According to my observations, you're doing well enough to leave immediately," I say in a stern voice. "You've no injuries."

He snarls at me. "Go to hell. I will stay here as long as I need."

I have no time for this. "We need the bed for injured patients. If you decide to stay any longer than tomorrow morning, you will have to find a spot for yourself on the cement floor." I point in the direction of the other room where our dying patients are laid and I say before walking away, "Though right now we can't even offer that." Nurses keep tending to them whenever they can, but we must use the spare beds for people that have a chance to survive.

I've noticed lately that Anna spends most of her time in that agonizing room. She holds their hands and talks to them. She knows that the nurses are way too busy helping the ones that still can be helped, so she devotes herself to those that are dying. I feel such respect for her and such pride that this amazing woman with an enormous heart is mine. She is my everything and helps me find strength. Without her nothing would make sense. I will do everything to keep her safe.

The next day is as busy as any other, so by the evening I'm so exhausted that I take a short break. I wander outside, hoping for some fresh air.

I head into the courtyard behind the ruined tenement, but someone's accented voice stops me. "Are you the doctor in this field hospital?"

I turn around to face a medium-height man with a friendly but guarded gaze. "Depends who is asking," I say, watching him with caution. You never know who might pretend to be one of our people while being a Nazi spy. His accent is the first indication to be alert.

"My name is Finn Keller," he answers. "I come here in peace as I'm Witek's friend. Are you the doctor on duty here? I will not talk to anyone else."

The moment he mentions Witek, a surge of pain rushes over me. I must find out what this is all about but I also must be cautious. "Are you German?" I ask without wasting any more time.

"You still didn't answer my question, but yes, I'm half German and half American."

I nod. "Yes, indeed, I'm the doctor here. What's this about?"

His mouth forms a slow smile. "Good because I have no more than a minute to spare. I was with Witek when he was killed." His eyes now reflect pure terror. "Anyway, I decided to stop here because he planned to visit this little hospital to warn the doctor here to watch out for a man named Leszek. That's all he said and I thought you would like to know this."

Witek probably saw Leszek and worried he would cause trouble. Thankfully, he left the hospital this morning. "Thank you. I appreciate it," I say.

He nods and turns away. "Keep safe."

"Did he suffer?" I ask after clearing my throat. This very question has bothered me since I learned the terrible news.

"No, it was an instant death." His voice is quiet. "He was the greatest man I've ever known."

THIRTY-SEVEN

LESZEK

He will pay for this. He made a fool out of me in front of everyone in this dirty hospital. I will leave but not before I take away from him what he values the most, just like he did to me all those years back. I've noticed the way he looks at her. Soon he will feel the very pain I've been feeling since Celina's death.

THIRTY-EIGHT

ANNA

31 August 1944

"Here you are." A savage voice from behind disturbs my thoughts and someone gently covers my eyes with his hands. "I've been waiting for this moment so long."

A sudden chill sweeps through my body the second my mind places the voice with the face. Leszek. The way he watched me during his stay at the hospital was very disturbing. It was a tremendous relief when he left. So, what is he doing here now?

The whole situation and his weird words make me push his hands away from my face but the moment I rise, he grabs my arm and thrusts me against the wall.

I strike my fists into his chest but he crushes me with his body and forces me even more into the wall. All I hear is the sound of my heartbeat thrashing in my ears as I scream for help. I doubt anyone can hear me since we are in the far corner of the courtyard behind the ruined tenement and there are constant artillery sounds in the distance.

I feel a pistol pressed to my chest. "Shut up or I will not

hesitate to kill you." He cocks his gun and adds, "You know I will do everything to take that smug smile from Odwaga's crooked mouth. I saw the way he looks at you."

"Let go of me," I whisper, afraid to make any louder sound. I know he isn't joking around and will not hesitate to shoot me. He already proved it the day he lied to Anzelm. "I did no wrong to you."

His face is so close to mine that I wince at the strong smell of canned sardines. "While I came back especially for you, I do admit you did no harm to me. I even admired your bravery at the café and now when you console those dying men in the hospital." He traces his finger across my ear. "Unfortunately, you must pay for your lover's deeds. Don't fret though, sweetheart, because you are about to learn what it means to be treated by a true man and not that flimsy Odwaga." He moves his free hand down and my spine stiffens when he jerks out the belt from his pants.

"You can't go on hating like this," I say, unable to stop my chin and lips from trembling.

He utters a gruff laugh. "He thinks he is better than all of us. He always treated me with pity and because of him, the love of my life died." He tightens his hold on me, restraining my breathing. "The only woman I ever loved... But I'm done discussing this with you. Let's have a little fun together, so Odwaga can cringe when he finds out. Then he will learn that the game is not over."

"Miss Anna, Doctor Odwaga needs you urgently." Hania's voice comes from the ruins. Every part of me tenses, expecting him to release the trigger of his gun before escaping.

Indecision flashes through his face. "Be silent or it will be your last breath," he whispers in my ear and stays put.

"I saw her going in the direction of the courtyard earlier, over there in the back," a male's voice rings out. It must be one of the patients. "Let me help you look for her, nurse."

"That would be great," Hania says and soon their footsteps get closer.

"*Kurwa mać!*" Leszek spits out the curse, pushes me away and bolts.

The unexpected release of tension washes through me. I feel dizzy and spent but focus on getting up before Hania and the other man arrive. Whatever just happened with Leszek was so unnerving that my body still shakes and my legs feel wobbly.

I get through the rest of the day without telling Mateusz about it. Leszek wanted to hurt me to weaken him. I must not let this happen. He is already exhausted because of lack of sleep and I don't want him to waste the rest of his energy on a miserable man like Leszek. One day I will tell him about it, but for now I trust him and I know whatever insults this awful man threw at him are not true.

We need our strength especially now, when the Old Town is about to capitulate and the Nazis will be here very soon. It's so hard to grasp what will happen next. It's been almost a month since Witek sent me to this underground hospital. What a hellish month, indeed. My entire focus has been on making sure we have enough food and water. It's become harder and harder as more damage has been caused by the Germans.

THIRTY-NINE

ANNA

The next day our patients and personnel are given permits to enter the underground sewers and escape with their squads to the city center. The fight over the Old Town is lost but one last crew is up there still fighting off the Nazis, so others can retreat to the sewers.

Mateusz sends off all our nurses to assist the wounded insurgents with their passage. But there are still some bedridden patients who did not get permits due to their condition. They are to stay here, and by the look at Mateusz's face, I dread that he's already decided on remaining here with them.

"Come on, Anna, you must leave now. The Germans will be here any moment." He points at the last insurgent climbing up the latter with his injured arm. "Fabian could use some of your help getting through the underground."

Fabian was one of our wounded patients and I saw him managing well on his own while escaping. "I'm staying here with you," I say in a choked voice and meet his feverish gaze. Red lines crowd the whites of his darting eyes but it's the amount of worry in them that tugs at my heart.

He shakes his head in denial. "You can't do that."

I cross my arms and lift my chin. "I can and I will. I'm responsible for this place whether you like it or not." It angers me how little faith he has in me. He thinks I'm going to scurry away like a little bunny and risk not seeing him anymore. No way.

He takes my face in his hands, and his gaze is now wet. "Darling, please run away before it's too late. I could never forgive myself if anything happened to you." He rubs my cheek with his fingers. "We don't know what they will do when they come here."

All my defiance evaporates in seconds. I rest my chin against his chest and whisper, "I'm staying here with you."

He wraps me in his embrace and kisses my forehead. "My stubborn Ania." His whisper is like a breath of fresh air. I exhale with relief sensing his defeat. He might be angry at me but he doesn't show it. Maybe it's sadness that plays in him right now, but whatever it is, we are staying together in this.

We check on the patients then sit on one of the abandoned beds, sharing a thin slice of black bread. It's still so quiet up there, just like before the explosion. Then a half an hour later a whisper comes from above.

We walk toward the sound and meet a pair of Fabian's brown eyes.

"Why aren't you with others?" Mateusz asks.

"Doctor Odwaga, you'd better leave now with me. The other part of the Old Town is already in German hands." He swallows loud. "They force people and our wounded brothers from basements and shoot them. I saw them throwing grenades into underground hospitals like this one and setting them in flames. You'd better take the nice lady and come with me now. The manhole is still open in here, but I bet not for long."

Mateusz's desperate gaze lands on me. "I can't leave these men but you must go with Fabian. There is still time." He shakes my shoulders. "This is not a game, Anna. It's about life and death."

I take a step back and shake my head with such force that my neck hurts.

He sighs and says, turning back to Fabian, "Before you leave, can you throw some debris on top of the entrance above us?"

"Will do," the man says before closing the top.

We hear some noises for a few minutes as true to his words, he tries to camouflage the hole.

Mateusz takes my hand and we walk toward the patients. "Listen all to me. Thankfully this hospital is in the ruins, so the Germans might not suspect we are even here. Let's be very silent."

Three men nod but the fourth one says, "Even if they don't find us here, we will die like rats."

"We have enough food to last us a few days if we ration," I say, trying to bring some hope into all of us.

"What will that do if you can't even escape with such blunderers like us?" He wipes sweat from his wrinkled forehead. He is in the worst condition of all as his both legs are amputated in efforts to save his life, and bandages wrap his head.

"He is right," a younger man with curly hair says. He pulls at Mateusz's arm. "Doctor, please have mercy on me and shoot me now, so I'm no longer a burden." His eyes are pleading. "I can't go on like this."

He has a chest injury but I know Mateusz believes he can fight it.

"Nonsense," Mateusz says. "We are in this together and we will do everything to survive." He touches his arm. "Try to be strong, boy. There are better days ahead of us." He winks at him.

"Doctor Odwaga is right," I say. "Our hospital is in ruins, so we have a high chance of not being spotted. Then we will find the way to leave." In this very moment I can't not think of the sisters from the convent. Will the Nazis kill them too? I know not all civilians were allowed to run through sewers and I doubt that the sisters even tried it. My heart goes out to them.

We remain in silence for the next couple of hours. I cling to Mateusz as we listen to any movement or commotion up there. By now all our squads are surely in the sewers.

First there are single shotguns in the far distance accompanied by submachines. Then the sounds get closer and closer and now we can hear shouts of people as well. Soon, Mateusz puts a finger to his mouth and we all are afraid to breathe. There are footsteps above us.

My spine stiffens as I listen to each and every noise.

Someone says in German, "Nothing here, just ruins."

I know the injured men don't understand German and probably are worrying now but I hope they obey Mateusz's request to be silent no matter what. I lean more into Mateusz and hold my breath.

"Yes, nothing here. Let's move to the next one," another man says and slams something straight into the entrance. Fabian must have done a good job throwing rubbish up there because nothing happens next.

Just when I'm about to exhale with relief, a terrible whimper escapes from behind us. I swirl around and find the younger insurgent shaking in convulsion.

Mateusz jumps toward him and holds him down, whispering something into his ear, slowly calming him down.

I want to cry because I sense that our cover is blown. Then I flinch at someone shouting in German, "Captain Arnold, someone is down there."

My stomach feels rock hard as they clear the entrance and one of them pokes his helmeted head in.

"It reeks like hospital," he says and retreats.

"You know the order: burn it." I'm so paralyzed that at first,

I miss the familiarity of this deep voice. Didn't another soldier call one of them "Arnold"? Same name and same voice. I must be right.

I spring to my feet and leap up. "Uncle Georg! It's me, Anna!" I use all my strength, so he can hear me.

"Anna," Mateusz's warning voice from behind makes me turn his way. "Stay away from the entrance or they will shoot you." He takes my hand and motions to step away.

I can't control my nervous laugh as I peer into his resigned face. He's already accepted the death sentence. I'm not angry at him this time, I'm just more determined than ever to act. It's a matter of minutes before the Nazis set the hospital alight while we are trapped here. "I'm trying to save us. Didn't you hear them?"

"Who's there?" a sharp voice rings from above.

I clear my throat and squeeze Mateusz's hand. "I'm Anna Otenhoff, a daughter of Fuhrer's prominent engineer, Francis Otenhoff. I would like to speak to my uncle Georg Arnold." I pray I'm not wrong and that he is indeed there. I feel like a little fly to be any moment attacked by a herd of long-legged spiders. I take the needed strength from Mateusz's touch.

"Who's there with you?" the same stranger asks. Even if Herr Arnold is there, he gives no indication. After all, he is not truly my uncle. As the dearest friend of my father, he visited our home often throughout my childhood. He gifted me with sweets and always took his time to play with me or tell me German legends. I got into the habit of calling him my "uncle."

"Only a doctor and four patients in critical condition," I say anticipating that they will tell me to go to hell and they will burn us alive.

But another voice shouts, "Step away from the ladder and raise your hands. All of you."

As we obey their command, two soldiers with submachines

walk down the ladder. I feel both sensations at the same time: paralyzing terror and a shard of hope.

They charge through the hospital as more soldiers join them. Everything is happening so fast and the whole situation is so nerve-wrecking that my mouth goes dry to the point I can't swallow.

But the tension in my muscles eases a bit at the sight of my *uncle* on the ladder even though he doesn't seem himself at all. It must be the effect of the uniform that makes him look so different to back then.

He takes me in and then moves to the surroundings. His face is rigid and hard, and so unreadable. He's a stranger now— one that orders destruction. This very realization crushes my heart with the force of an elephant foot as his words play in my mind, *You know the order: burn it.*

I try not to flinch as he keeps examining me with his piercing-blue eyes. My gut tells me that whatever comes next will poison my blood and doom all of us. The hope I felt just before slowly transforms into anger, as it did with my father. But my father loves me while this man is just a stranger who can easily overlook the past. How is it possible that people change like this? Does war have this type of power to ruin the kindest man into a monster? War is like a clinical trial lining us up and checking our responses. It flashes out our true characters and tendencies; it defines us as human beings.

"It is truly you, my Anna," he says making me go completely still. He sounds just like the old, warm uncle, if only it weren't for that wicked look in his face. "I didn't expect to see you in a rat hole like this one." His last words crush any remaining hope. He's like the others.

I lift my chin and hold his gaze without a single blink. "It's a hospital, Uncle Georg. I can assure you that we saved the lives of many German soldiers here as well."

His face muscles seem to soften. "You sound just like your

beloved Mutti. Francis still misses her." He stares into the floor like he is trying to resolve some sort of issue. "Well, I met with your papa right before leaving for Warsaw. He made me promise that I would find you and convince you to go back to Berlin. I looked in your café and other places," he frowns and shrugs his shoulders, "and for millions of years, this dungeon is the last place I would consider finding you."

I know explaining things to him would only worsen my situation. After all, I'm at a Polish hospital and at his mercy. I stay silent.

"I don't have to tell you this is not a good place to be in right now. We all have to execute the order issued by the Führer himself to turn this city into ashes."

His admission sends chills up my spine. I want to shout at him that this is not right. This city is already stained with blood and now they are committing even more slaughters. I want to call him a murderer. It takes all my resolve not to do it. At the same time, I know that only staying silent or saying lies can save us. I choose the first—the lesser evil.

I decide to be direct with him. "Do you have to kill us too, Uncle Georg?" I suppress my tears. I would not give him that satisfaction, but I know that if I must beg him to save Mateusz's life, I will not hesitate.

He gives me a troubled look. "How could you think of me like this, my Anna? I have too much fondness for you, besides I promised Francis to keep you safe should our paths cross." He sighs. "I'm so glad I came just in time." He peruses Mateusz and the bedridden men like he's seeing them for the first time. "Not too many of them left, huh?" he adds with contempt.

I can't help but let hope slip into my heart even though I feel like a traitor. Why should we have the privilege of staying alive if there are so many innocent people in this Old Town that are being hunted and murdered? But the will to live is strong in me and so I quietly accept his mercy.

"Let's get you out of here," he says and extends his hand to touch my arm.

The same moment he does it, I take a step back. "I'm not going without these good men," I say.

His lips press together, flattening, as he narrows his eyes. "You're taking an unnecessary risk. After we leave, there will be other troops here with the same assignment. You will all be burned alive."

"Not if you help us, as you promised my father," I say and give him a meaningful look. He can't walk out on us just like that, not when he has the power to help us.

His voice is quiet and tense now. "I promised to save you, Anna, not a herd of damn Poles," he says through his clenched teeth.

"Please, Uncle Georg, help us. As I told you, we saved so many German soldiers in this hospital."

He runs his fingers through his curly mustache. "Only on one condition."

I resume my breathing again. He just gave me a sliver of hope. "And that is?" I ask.

"I will organize a transport for you and your *friends*." He spits the last word. "Transport to our hospital outside of Warsaw where these men will get the right care." He licks his dry lips. "But you will immediately leave to Berlin. You must promise to go along with that." He rakes his eyes over my face as if trying to detect a hint of disagreement.

"Yes, I promise to do just that," I say without hesitation. Promising anything to this murderer means nothing to me and I will have no issue breaking it, if it comes to it.

"I'm glad to help you, my Anna. Take better care of yourself," he says before turning and walking away. He tells one of his soldiers to leave someone on guard up there, so other troops won't assault us.

I close my eyes, trying to overcome the hollowness in my chest. I feel like I just made a deal with the devil himself.

From behind, Mateusz puts his hands around my waist and I lean into him. "Thank you for doing this for us," he whispers, tickling my ear.

"It doesn't matter," I whisper back as tears roll down my cheeks. "There are too many here that can't be saved."

"It's a sign from God." He runs his hand through my hair. "He wants us to stay alive."

"You sound like Sister Dorota." The moment I say it, dread lands in my stomach. "What has happened to her and the other sisters? Are they still alive?" I turn and hold his gaze.

In response he pulls me closer. "I don't know, darling, but the only thing I'm certain of is that you found a way of doing the impossible and saving us." His broken voice fills all the angles of pain within me.

FORTY

MATEUSZ

1 September 1944, a small village outside of Warsaw

Watching Anna peacefully sleep beside me is a very foreign thing. While at the hospital, sleep became a luxury we couldn't afford. We stole a few hours here and there, but it was never a peaceful kind of rest.

In this tiny room, on this straw-mattress bed, things seem so simple, as if everything we went through never happened, as if there is no fight boiling in our beloved city. Now when she is in good hands, I must go back there to continue our battle. I could not look at myself in the mirror if I stayed here while they struggle over there.

Warsaw is encircled by German soldiers, so no Poles can enter it to help out in this uneven fight. But I know there are ways to sneak in. I will go through the Kampinos Forest. I know the area around the city very well thanks to numerous pre-war hiking and camping trips with the scouts and later with friends. I must find a way to get from there to the city center and join my brothers and sisters. I don't care that we no longer have a chance of winning. It's a matter of honor and duty to not abandon them in this critical moment.

Yet, leaving Anna is torture. I wish for fate not to part us anymore but some things are unavoidable. I would never risk taking her with me as the chance of being caught and executed is incredibly high. I didn't tell her about my plans because she would never agree to stay behind. There is still a risk that she will try to get into Warsaw on her own once she discovers that I left, but I also sense she may know better not to. She doesn't know the area that well and no one is being let into the burning city.

I brush away a strand of hair from her face and listen to her deep breathing. I memorize every detail in her face, so it stays fresh in my mind for as long as we stay apart, maybe for eternity. Her beautiful rosy lips are so inviting but I know I can't wake her. It's almost time to go, so I gently kiss her forehead and inhale the lavender scent of soap Pani Maria gave us to wash ourselves.

It was a long, exhausting day. At one point, I was sure we were going to die when the German soldiers discovered us. But Anna found a way to save us. I still believe it's God's doing to send that Nazi she knew during her childhood to our hospital. The moment there was an opportunity to act, she took advantage of it. She proved once more that there is a way even in the most hopeless moments.

I admire her determination and cleverness. She recognized the voice of a man she hadn't seen for years and didn't hesitate for a moment to expose herself, so our survival was possible.

I couldn't stand even looking at the man but I knew better than to interfere. It was safer when he thought I was just a doctor who didn't understand a word from their exchange. But it pained me to no end watching Anna be so vulnerable in front of this Nazi monster. I sensed her true thoughts and that she was ready to spit in the man's face. I sensed the struggle within her because I know her well.

But my Ania is strong and restrained herself from the act that would doom all of us. She skillfully played a lost woman that needed the bastard's help. She used the connection from the past to achieve her goal even as she ached for all the people killed after the Germans ascended the Old Town.

True to the man's words, within two hours a tarpaulin-covered truck arrived. Soon we were on our way, sitting with our patients on the stretchers at the back of the lorry. The vehicle was operated by a German soldier with bloodshot eyes. Another man sat beside him, more accurately, he slept beside him. The fight takes a toll also on our enemy despite our impressions of how robotic they are.

At some point the truck began driving slowly, so I took a peek outside. Two cars before us there was a patrol checking documents. That was when Anna convinced me to escape. She reasoned that the soldiers already had an order to bring the men to the hospital, so our absence would not make a difference for them. We knew she was to immediately depart for Berlin by transportation organized by her Nazi *uncle*, but we didn't know what they would do with me. It was damn hard to abandon the wounded men but I agreed with Anna that we had no choice.

It was easy to jump out and run into fields. The two soldiers didn't even notice as there were no shotguns in our wake. To our luck, there were no other vehicles behind us.

Soon I was able to determine our location and knew that not far from there is a small village where Pani Maria lives with her son. My family visited them often before the war because my mother liked to buy poultry and eggs from them.

When she opened the door of her wooden cottage, it took me a moment to be sure it was the same lady. Deep wrinkles covered her face and strands of gray hair stuck out from her dark-green head covering. She on the other hand recognized me right away because without a word she ushered us inside.

"I trust my neighbors, they are good people, but one never knows," she said once we were standing in the tiny foyer. "So, you became a doctor like your father." She eyed my blood-stained apron. "Are you coming from the uprising?" She whispered the last words. She pressed her hand to her lips as if trying not to let out a sob of despair. "My son is there too."

"We are coming from the Old Town. It was lost but our people still fight in the city center and Żoliborz."

"I pray every day for all of you. But please come to the kitchen. You must be hungry and I just made potato dumplings."

Her words made my stomach grumble as I introduced Anna. We had a tasty supper and learned more about Pani Maria's son Wojtek who left home to join the uprising. She was in her mid-seventies and she complained about her struggles managing the small steading of one cow and some hens. She still had fields to maintain and potatoes that needed to be harvested. Anna promised we would help and Pani Maria offered the room in her home.

After supper we washed ourselves and went straight to bed, which the kind lady had made for us. She must have assumed we were wife and husband.

Even the hard and poky mattress seemed a luxury after not sleeping in a bed for so long. We curled under the wool cover and kissed for a long time, before falling asleep.

Now, hours later, it's time to leave the woman I love more than words can describe. I don't know if she will ever forgive me, but I know it's the right thing to do. Damn hard, but right.

FORTY-ONE

ANNA

30 September 1945, Warsaw

Even though the war officially ended months ago, this country is far from being independent. It went from one oppressor to another. While Stalin's regime rules Poland now, there are many who have never accepted it. One of them is my Mateusz who lives with partisans in forests now from where they fight the regime.

That morning a year ago when I woke to him being gone, the uncontrolled anger perplexed me. The reality that he left me behind made me choke. I tried entering the city pretending to be a German nurse ready to help wounded Nazi soldiers. I wanted to find a way to join the fight in the city center, and I was sure that's where Mateusz was headed. But at this point no one was allowed in.

I went back to Pani Maria and for the next month I helped her in the household. When we heard that the uprising had ended due to the capitulation signed by the Polish side, I dreaded the worst. I knew Mateusz was either gone or in captivity, so when he showed up at Pani Maria's door, I felt no more anger toward him, just elation. He was able to mix with citizens and escape the transport to the POW camps in Germany.

At the beginning Mateusz had to be in hiding because the Nazis were going through villages looking for insurgents who were able to escape after the uprising.

We stayed together in Pani Maria's home for months. Even though I still had so many worries about the future, I consider that time one of the best in my life. I was gifted those months with the man I love so fiercely. At first, I had this hope in me that after the war we would go back to Warsaw and build our life from scratch. I thought there was nothing more important than being together.

Mateusz on the other hand, went through constant aches for his hurting homeland. It was always on his mind to the point he suffered from insomnia. That's when I knew that one day, we would go our separate ways. So, when the war officially ended in May of this year, leaving Poland in Stalin's hands, Mateusz made his decision to join partisans and fight against the new regime. He believes that there is a chance for a third world war to happen which would free Poles from the clutches of Soviets.

It was painful letting him go but I knew I had no choice. All I could do was support him in his decision. But deep in me I wish he had made a different choice, one that would include me at his side. During those months we engaged in endless conversations about what needed to be done once the war ended, and always the need for rebuilding Warsaw came first. Why can't he be here with me helping this broken city to rise again?

And as much as my heart has never stopped aching since losing him, every day I find a new strength to keep going. I want to believe that one day all of this will end and he will be back to me, but I know better than to be naïve. Once he chose to go against the system, his life could never be normal again.

I decided not to go back to Germany as I feel my true home

is here. It's where I became independent and happy again; it's where I met the love of my life; it's where I fought when my own nation, driven by a lunatic, turned against life and basic human values.

My tenement got partially destroyed during the uprising but I moved in anyway in hopes for it to be rebuilt one day. Many people did the same once they returned to Warsaw—they live in not wholly ruined buildings. Some parts of Warsaw were destroyed more than others. The Old Town was in ashes left by the Nazis.

Soon after I came back to Warsaw, I joined the cast at the Powszechny Theater. So far, I've performed in *The Morality of Mrs. Dulska*, a play by Gabriela Zapolska. I love being back in my profession again. It gives me such pleasure and fulfillment.

In my free time I help clearing the debris away in the city, since every pair of hands matters. It's what I've been doing for the last several hours. I regret that I decided to walk back home as I'm having a hard time ignoring my body aches. What I dream of is a warm bath and hot tea before collapsing into my bed. But it's all worth it because the satisfaction I feel every time I help brings peace to me. We can't change the past, but we can work on improving the future. Warsaw will be rebuilt and being a part of this process is important to me. I hate Stalin's regime and the fact that Poland didn't get back its independence but my way of fighting it is by helping rebuild it because one day this country will be free from the oppressor.

There are a lot of bad things happening right now and innocent people who fought for this country are hunted down and harassed. The reality that one day I might be one of them scares me to death.

The sight of a tall, gray-haired man in an elegant black suit standing at my door and holding a little boy's hand, jerks me from my reverie. Who would be visiting so late? As I get closer, the man turns his stern, familiar face at me. I fumble.

What is Helmut's father doing here? He is the last person I would expect to see. But he is right before me, measuring me with his cold gaze. During the short time I lived with Helmut, his father's frosty demeanor was something we dealt with every day. But he was a man of few words and he always treated me with respect. I sometimes wondered if he knew that Helmut abused me. If he did, he never gave any indication of it.

"Hello, Anna," he says in a quiet voice.

"Hello, Herr von Liberchen. I didn't expect to see you here."

"I'm so sorry to be bothering you so late but it's important I talk to you before we go back to Germany tomorrow morning." The moment the boy turns his head my way, a bitter tang settles in my mouth. It's as if Helmut looks at me from his face. I look back at my father-in-law to regain my composure. This little boy with extremely gaunt features, who looks no more than five, is Helmut's son.

The initial shock makes way for empathy for this boy. The fact that he is alive after all brings such peace to my heart. "Of course, please come in." I unlock the door and gesture for them to step inside, to the untouched half of the tenement where my tiny apartment is situated.

I point to the sofa and ask, "Would you like something to drink before I go wash myself?" I can't possibly be conversing while I'm all caked in dust.

They settle on the sofa and Helmut's father puts his arm around the little boy. "Please take your time. We will gladly wait here," he says.

I kneel in front of the boy and smile. "Would you like some cocoa?"

His shy gaze shows excitement. "Yes, miss."

After I hand the warm drink to the boy, I go to the bathroom and wash my face in the sink. Thankfully I remembered to wear a head covering, so I don't have to spend an endless time combing debris dust from my hair like the other day.

When I return to my guests, the boy is asleep on the sofa while the man stands at the window with his back to me.

I go to my bedroom to grab my woolen blanket and then return to cover the boy with it. I kiss his forehead and sit next to him. Despite the fact that he reminds me so much of Helmut, my heart goes out to him. Ruth, his mother, is not here, and that speaks a lot of this boy's situation and what he went through.

Helmut's father now watches me from across the room while resting in my armchair. "I see you're already fond of my grandchild." A gentle smile tugs at his mouth making him look so different.

"He has Helmut's eyes." My statement just hangs there for a short moment while we avert our gazes.

"I hate taking much of your time as I can see how tired you are." He motions to the boy. "Let me start with the story of this little boy, as you are family and you deserve to know it."

I nod, curious about what happened to his mother. In truth, I'm touched by his words and it's not until now I sense there is a huge change in this man. Maybe he was always like this but I failed to see it.

"Last week I received a call from the orphanage in Warsaw where Peter had stayed. Ruth, his mother, perished in Auschwitz death camp but he survived by sheer luck."

While he stares down for a long moment, I stay silent as well. Ruth is gone.

He clears his throat. "The Red Cross found me because Peter has our family name even though as you know Helmut never married Ruth. She never told the boy the truth about his father. He thinks that he was a war hero..." Another long moment of a heavy silence. It seems as if he's trying to use as few words as possible to give me all the information. Then he continues in a monotonous voice, "The very sad news is that no one survived from Ruth's side of the family." He bends forward, laying his head on his arms.

I dig into my pocket and take out a tissue to wipe my tears. "There are so many that perished..."

"Yes. I want you to know that I never took part in what happened. I never signed for the Nazi party," he slumps his shoulders, "but some say that silence could be as evil."

I still remember his conversations with my father about the Nazis. Papa was upset with him for not joining the movement but he overlooked his point of view and the fact that he called Adolf Hitler as heretic, simply because Papa thought that Helmut was a perfect candidate for my husband.

"Anyway, Helmut signed up and was recruited by the Gestapo as he was afraid that they would take everything away from us. You know, I was home that day he called and gave Ruth and Peter up to the Gestapo. I was furious with him. I knew about his double life and I let him have it because I saw how happy it made him. He was productive and finally responsible, helping run the brewery. I was so proud of him, so when he betrayed the family he loved so much, I couldn't understand why." He takes out a cigar. "Would you mind me smoking?"

"Go ahead," I say.

After exhaling a cloud of smoke, he goes on, "Later I learned that he was forced to do it. He signed a written agreement with them that as long as he served as a Gestapo agent, Ruth and Peter would remain safely in one of the camps in Germany. This stayed true until February of 1944, a month after Helmut's death."

I have a hard time accepting this revelation. I clear my throat. "Helmut was serious when it came to fulfilling his job duties. He worked here in Warsaw at the Gestapo headquarters on Szucha Avenue where he tortured innocent Poles and ordered massive executions." I want him to know this because criminals like Helmut deserved no praise. Yes, he managed to save his family but at the same time was so ruthless toward others. Maybe he just wanted so badly to climb the ladder to his career in the Nazi circle that he forgot how to be a decent human.

Sorrow settles in his eyes as he avoids my gaze. "I know all about it. There is no day when I don't pray for his victims. I'm not trying to justify his acts, but I take significant blame for the way he was lost in this life and for his poor decisions. Now I know I was too strict, always busy with the family business and never having time for my children. My wife did terrible things while I was away and unfortunately Helmut witnessed her cheating on me with other men. It took a huge toll on him, and when she retired to her room and shut down the world around her, it affected him even more." He sighs. "And I didn't know how to show compassion to my children, especially Helmut. I believed that if I was hard on him, he would one day abandon his weaknesses for gambling and women and become responsible. But it was Ruth he changed for. I ruined his happiness by forcing him to marry you." He gives me a long and meaningful look. "I need to apologize to you for this too."

"My father wanted the same," I say.

"Yes, I know. I'm telling you all of this, so you understand that my son wasn't a bad person all the way through. But yes, he made poor choices and he fully deserves to be blamed for the tragedy of so many people. I suspect he committed all these terrible things because he wanted to gain enough importance to be able to one day keep Ruth and Peter. Still, that explanation is of no relevance."

"I understand what you are trying to say. I wish things went differently."

"I'm determined not to make the same mistake while raising Peter. I love him more than words can describe and I will make sure he always knows this."

"He's lucky to have you," I say, trying to shake off all the sorrow his story brought on.

"I'm the lucky one. Inga can't wait to welcome him into our home. By the way, she sends hugs."

My memories of Helmut's sister are fond as she always treated me with compassion. "Thank her, please. How is she?"

His tired face shows a ray of sunshine. "She's doing well. She's been invaluable help running the estates. This is actually why I'm here, to assure you that our home is always open to you. You'll always be part of our family." He reaches for his leather bag and takes out a set of paperwork from folder. "Here, I need your signature on these documents. I set up an account under your name with a wealthy amount. It's the least I can do for you."

Once more this man surprises me. I can't imagine taking any of Helmut's money though. "This is so kind of you, Mr. von Liberchen, but—"

He waves his hand at me. "Please don't reject it as it may come in handy one day. It will be there until the day you need it. This is something I care tremendously to do for you since I can't change the past and my mistakes. I never signed any of our assets under Helmut's name because I was afraid he would sell it all. Now, when I have a grandchild, I'm at peace knowing he will inherit it one day."

When I gaze at the document in my hand, I gasp at the large number. "Are you certain you're comfortable doing this?"

"Yes. I know this can't justify what you went through while being abused by my son, but at least it's something I can do to make your life easier."

FORTY-TWO

ANNA

20 August 1947, Tosaki, a village in north-eastern Poland

I don't know why I'm even here standing at the door of Wanda's aunt. The wooden cottage looks as enchanted as she described to me a long time ago. Once it was a large garden surrounding the manor home but now everything seems in disarray. Weeds and tall grass over grow the colorful flowers and bushes that I'm sure were once well taken care of. If not for the chirping birds and dogs barking in the far distance, I would wonder if anyone even lives here.

But the moment I tap on the door with brown paint peeling off, an elderly woman with gray hair and a soft-wrinkled face opens it.

"Hello," I say. "My name is Anna Otenhoff and I'm Wanda's friend from Warsaw. I was in the area, so I thought I would stop to say hello."

The inquiring expression on her face changes into a welcoming one. "Oh, yes, Wanda told me a lot of good things about you. Please come in."

When I enter, a whiff of warm air swaddles me and I enjoy breathing in a sweet vanilla scent.

"Let's take a seat at the kitchen table as I just baked a blueberry pie," Wanda's aunt says and leads me toward a small table covered by a gingham-blue cloth. The interior décor is modest with thrifty items consisting of a small sofa in the living room and a round table with a set of chairs. There are also some bookshelves decorated with framed photos. It's hard to believe that Wanda's aunt and uncle belong to nobility.

We eat the blueberry pie and drink tea while having a casual conversation. "Once the Soviets came, they took over our manor house and we had no choice but remain in this gardener's cottage," she says with a sigh. "Our whole estate was permanently taken away from us and parceled. They make everything public. We are only left with this cottage and a strip of land."

"I'm so sorry to hear this," I say. "You lost everything."

She waves her hand. "We are old, so we don't need much and we don't have children." She sighs again. "It's still hard to accept it. I was hoping that my nephew would take it over one day and continue the family tradition but now it's too late."

"Would you happen to know where I can find your nephew?" The moment I ask, her face gains a guarded look.

"No, I haven't seen him at all."

I reach across the table and take her hand in mine. "Look, Mrs. Gratowska, you do not need to worry. I've decided to move abroad as living in this corrupt country is impossible for an actress like me, unless I share their propaganda." I wave a fly away from my hand and continue, "I wanted to say goodbye to Mateusz before leaving. That's all. I promise."

"I believe you, my child. Wanda trusts you, so why wouldn't I? Mateusz shows up once in a while but we never know when it's going to be. You see, UB, Stalin's Security Service, is after him, they even distributed posters with his picture on it, so he must be very careful."

I knew Mateusz belonged to the partisans and fights with the current system hiding in the woods. I knew they attacked UB prisons and do everything to go against Stalin's regime but I had no idea that the system was so intensely after him. "So, there is no way I can find him now?"

Why don't you stay here with us for a couple of days and I will see if I can contact him? How does that sound?"

I'm not in any rush at all and the opportunity to stay out in the country is so enticing that I say, "I would love to but only if it's truly no trouble."

"No, not at all. My husband is out working in the fields all day, so I appreciate the company." She smiles. "You see, my dear husband finds no better happiness than out in nature."

"Thank you for your kindness," I say and smile back at her. "I see all the nice things Wanda said about you are true."

"Oh, my dear Wanda. How I miss her. I wish she would visit more but I understand she has a lot on her plate now." She sighs. "Anyway, there is the Narew river not far from here if you like swimming. Wanda adores it and always spends so much time basking in the sun and swimming when they visit. Just watch out and don't wander too far as it's still not safe around here."

Wanda's uncle comes over in the late evening and is as kind as her aunt. My dear friend always talks about him as her beloved Wujek Mirek. A large gray dog remains at his side the whole time. He reminds me of a wolf but only when it comes to his looks because he is so playful and wags his tail at me. When I learn his name is *Wilczur*, Wolfie, I can't suppress my laugh.

We eat *placki ziemniaczane,* potato pancake, for supper and drink milk. He is a quiet man visibly tired after a whole day of hard labor. His calloused hands don't indicate that once he was so wealthy. I don't sense any pretense from him or bitterness even though he has plenty of reasons for both. The pro-war regime despoiled him from everything. Yet, the moment he entered his home, there was only a smile on his face and a warm kiss for his wife to whom he speaks with tremendous respect. He reminds me so much of my late maternal grandfather from Germany. He was the same, a hard-working and kind man, and I know deep in my heart that he would never have supported the Nazi ideology. Never.

~

The next morning, I go for a walk but before I leave, Wanda's aunt promises to let me know as soon as she is able to get in touch with Mateusz.

For a city girl like myself, contact with nature seems a rare treat. As I cross a long meadow, I listen to birds chirping up in the crowns of birch trees and inhale a tint of hay in scorching sun. I have this weird sensation of someone watching me. I look around but there is no one here, so I waddle through tall grass populated with yellow, white and purple flowers. Still, I could swear that someone follows me. Wanda's aunt said not to wander too far because the area is still not safe, so I take a narrow dirt path up the high ground with walls of osier on both sides. And there it is—a sandy dune.

When I reach the beach, the view of the twisted river and complexes of large trees on the other side of the shore take my breath away. The stream of river burbling over the nearest rocks puts my mind into a delicious laziness. I enjoy the fishy and musky scent. It is all so relaxing. It's so tempting to forget about the whole world and live right here in this moment within the virgin beauty of nature. Now I understand why Wanda so adores this place.

After prolonged admiration of the landscape, I lie on the sand and observe white clouds moving through the peaceful blue sky. Like us humans, they keep going without pausing and appreciating the beauty of present time. I close my eyes to tune in with the surroundings, my mind so lethargic. So when I hear Mateusz's whisper above me, "Ania, you're here," I know I'm already dreaming. I want to hear more and more of that delightful sound. I want to dream only about him, as always.

But when I feel the touch of his fingers on my cheek, I open my eyes. "Is it really you?" I whisper, still unable to grasp his closeness, my nerves firing all at once.

We gaze at each other so intensely that I forget to blink. He brushes a strand of hair away from my forehead. "My beautiful Ania, how I missed you."

For a moment I wonder if this bearded man with a gaunt face, dressed in shabby clothes is truly my Mateusz. Only his voice and hazel eyes betray him. "How I missed you," I say and run my hand through his hair.

He presses his finger to my lips. "Shhh..." Then his mouth crashes into mine sending jolts of hot sparkles through my heart. I part my lips but for a second, we just breathe each other in like we waited for this moment for eternity. His lips are soft and taste salty, and that's when I realize there are tears rolling down his cheeks.

As my own tears emerge, I want to tell him tender words of my love but the kiss intensifies consuming my body and tormenting my soul. I want this moment to never end and I wish we could die right now, in this entangle of love.

My heart beats faster and faster as he works his urgent mouth against mine. The world doesn't exist anymore, only his overpowering masculinity. For the first time in my life, I'm voluntarily dominated by a man and it brings me completeness.

But when he breaks the kiss, a plunge of disappointment soars through me. He sits upright and puts hands over his face. "I'm sorry. I've no right."

I touch his arm. "Mateusz, I came here to find you."

"Look at me. I have nothing to offer and probably will be dead soon. You're better off staying away."

"Don't say that." I move closer, put my arms around him and rest my chin on his shoulder. "It's still not too late. We can go to England and make a life together."

"I wish that was possible. But I'm doomed with this broken fatherland. My destiny is to stay here and fight to the end."

"Fight for what? Don't you understand the battle is over? The truth is that we lost it a long time ago and the quicker you understand it, the more chance you have to survive, to live."

He springs to his feet and stays facing the river. "Of everyone, I always thought you would understand it." The pain in his voice brings tears to my eyes.

"You know I understand it. I just can't watch you dying for the cause that no longer exists. We lost the fight the moment the uprising failed. There is nothing else we can do besides staying alive and wait it away."

He turns back, his eyes red now as he breathes loud. "Wait it away? Watch my homeland turn into Stalin's puppet? Do you really think it's the only thing we can do?"

I avert my eyes from his hot gaze and say in a quiet voice, "Yes, I think it's the most sensible thing to do... to make the best out of it." My pulse speeds up while I contain the growing anger within me. Why does he have to be so narrow minded? "For God's sake, Mateusz, I'm not asking you to join the party and be one of them. I just ask you to be sensible and stay alive because the way you're heading now is straight to a graveyard." I hate being so blatant but I have no choice if I want to have the slightest chance of convincing him. "I'm not asking you to betray your homeland, I only want you to stay alive because the fight is already over."

His face is all red now as he's pacing back and forth. "You're wrong. There is still so much we can do. Don't you see what is happening?" he says in a raised voice. "They throw us in prisons and slaughter us like pigs." He kneels in front of me, his face so close I can smell the woodsy scent that emanates from him.

"Everyone who ever fought for this country is treated equally as a criminal. But of course, the official verdict is espionage or some other bullshit. This is the injustice we are fighting. And as long as we don't stop, there will be a chance for a third war. That's the only way to make things right." His voice is softer and softer as he continues, "So don't tell me the fight is over because I will never accept it."

In this moment I know with all my heart that he will not change his mind. I'm so desperate, though, that I say, "What about us? I love you and want to have a future with you. Does that mean nothing to you?"

His eyes darken with pain as he strokes my cheek with his palm. "It means everything to me, and you know it." His words choke with emotion. "Words can't describe what I feel for you."

The damn tears will not stop as my heart grasps his words and the tender way he said them. "Then come with me." My voice cracks because I already know the answer. "I'm leaving tomorrow morning."

Silently, he takes me in his embrace and we stay like this for a long time. I try to carve into my memory the way his touch feels, the way his lips take mine like it's the last time. I can hear the hammering in his chest that matches my own. We both know it's the last moment we'll share together. My body is limp and I have no strength to break this embrace even though I'm so angry at him, even though my sadness intensifies. And as much as I'm angry at him, I love him so fiercely that it takes my breath away. It's so hard because his love is as clear as the summer sky.

On my way back to the cottage, I'm so numb that I feel like I'm walking in darkness. I've lost all hope. He's the love of my life, and my days will turn cold without him.

I must tell Wanda's aunt that I have a headache and need to lie down. This will allow me time alone, so I can mend my broken heart to the point to go on with my life. I note a car parked upfront but I don't even have the strength to glance its way. I walk in expecting to encounter the nice lady but instead there are uniformed men jumping my way the moment I enter.

They take a hold of me and one of them shouts, "You're arrested." Then he turns to Wanda's aunt and says, "You lied to us and deserve the punishment."

Everything happens so fast that in my numbness I realize too late that it's the UB taking me in their clutches. They finally decided to go after me. But why here? Maybe it's better that way because right now I would rather die than go on without Mateusz. After all that, I'm destined to share his unavoidable fate.

FORTY-THREE

LESZEK

This time she won't run away from me. I will use her to get to that bastard Odwaga. I've been waiting for this moment since the war ended. He's a sneaky fox and so far, none of my troops have been able to capture him.

Of course, I could use his aunt to get to him but my mama made me promise to never do any harm to this old woman. I've so much love for my mama that I will honor her wish. She raised me to be a good man and now she can be proud of me.

"Take him to his cell," I say to the guard and point at the bearded man on the floor covered in blood. I've been so occupied with my thoughts that I didn't notice when he fainted from the whipping, I treated him with. "Bring him back tomorrow morning. Maybe his tongue will untwist by then."

This damn job is so tiring. No one appreciates what I do. Not even my family. Last year I married a daughter of the chief of this prison.

We have a three-month old son who looks just like me. Even though I feel nothing for his mother, I adore my little boy. I will teach him how to survive in this treacherous world and that he cannot trust anyone. He will know that people are snakes.

Once, I had so much trust thanks to my gentle mother. She kept teaching me that I must help others and we prayed every night for the poor. But this noble way of hers brought her to her grave. The woman she called her dearest friend betrayed her and made her vulnerable to the Gestapo. That changed me forever. I will make sure that my son will not make the same mistake.

But right now, what I need to do is use that German bitch to lead me to Odwaga. It might not be easy as she is clever. I noticed it many times during the war. I'm convinced though that my whip will perform its job well.

FORTY-FOUR

MATEUSZ

I turn the rabbit on a spit over the bonfire while trying to get back to reality. Since seeing Anna yesterday, I can't focus on the smallest tasks, so I was assigned the temporary duties of the cook for our unit.

It's so hard to digest the fact that it was most likely the last time I will see her. I do take comfort in knowing she will go abroad and begin a new life. I'm proud as hell that she refused to be Stalin's puppet and spread their garbage. She is a very talented actress and she will have a chance at a good career in England, unlike here.

It drained me seeing her tears and it nearly made me change my mind about staying. I thought about leaving all of this and going with her instead. But I would not be able to look at myself in the mirror for the rest of my life. Some duties are sacred, including the responsibility to keep fighting for our homeland. I won't stop until they drain the last drop of my blood from me. I saw in Anna's eyes that she understood, despite her words, but she didn't accept it. She deserves someone better anyway, not a simple doctor with no future in his own fatherland. I'm cursed and I would only drag her down with me. There is nothing that would pain me more than seeing her share my fate.

It's enough that I've already lost my father. There isn't a day when I don't blame myself for it. At the time, when Witek said that the best thing would be to stay away from Warsaw and keep my family in the dark about my affairs, it seemed so sensible. I hoped it was enough to keep my loved ones protected. But how mistaken I was. That night when Tata died, they came looking for me. They demanded he tell them where they could find me. If he had told them, maybe they would have spared him. But he couldn't because he simply didn't know. I doubt though that he would have told them even if he knew.

My father was a very brave man unlike myself. He never hesitated when it came to taking risks, not before or during the war. Mama often got so upset with him because of that. He made a lot of mistakes in his life, but he also did a lot of good. He had a huge heart and an open mind. I think Wanda got it from him, as she never turns back once she is committed to something. I wonder if there will ever be a time in my life when I get used to the pain of losing him.

"Odwaga, I've been looking everywhere for you," Jakub, a large, blond boy from my squad says while sitting beside me. "What the hell are you doing cooking the rabbit?"

"I'm not sure myself," I say and chuckle. "Don't fret. You're in for the best feast ever."

He sighs. "I don't doubt it. It seems whatever you work on is impeccable." He touches my arm. "Listen, friend, I hate to spoil your good mood but I have a message."

My mouth goes dry. "Is it about my aunt and uncle?" I would never forgive myself if something happened to them. Because of me they are in danger too. It's how I learned about Anna's visit. I went to do one of my checks on them, to make sure they weren't in trouble, when I saw her leaving Ciocia Krysia's and Wujek Mirek's cottage. I couldn't believe my eyes.

An instant longing overpowered me, to the point where I followed her like a lovesick fool.

"They're fine. Your aunt sent a message through my girl. Anna was arrested by UB and taken to Bialystok."

Heat rises behind my eyelids as I grab his arm. "Are you sure?"

He nods. "That's all she told me."

I spring to my feet and bolt away, unable to sort my thoughts. The stab of pain that hits me makes my legs shaky. Not my Anna, not her. Is it because she stayed at ciocia's and that made them suspect her of cooperating with me? I knew she refused to go along with the Soviet regime but if they left her alone for so long, why would they go after her now? Maybe someone informed them that she planned to flee abroad? My head is spinning from all the unanswered questions.

I stop running through the forests only when I can find no more breath. I lean against a tree and try to sort my thoughts. I must find a way of getting her out. The fact that she was taken straight to Białystok is not a good sign. If she was arrested and kept somewhere here, we could try freeing her by attacking the post. Getting into Białystok prison is harder than getting into Szucha during the war. They take extreme measures to ensure no one can get inside.

Just the thought of what they will put her through squeezes my stomach into a knot. My beautiful innocent Anna is at the mercy of the worst men in the country and I'm not able to help her. I think and think, and I'm near going insane when I remember Zdzisiek. I saw him a couple of months ago in Warsaw for a brief moment when visiting Mama and the family. It was before they hung posters with my face all over Poland.

Zdzisiek was a great leader during the war and the uprising but now he'd decided to go with the flow and join the ruling party saying that it's the best thing in this situation that one can do for Poland. According to him, the fighting under partisans makes no sense anymore and it's better to accept the current situation in hopes of times changing in favor for Poles. I don't agree with his stand but maybe he can find a way of helping me since he belongs to the communist party?

As much as I despise myself for even taking this route, I'm so desperate and I would do anything for Anna. Anything. It's only now I understand the full extent of my feelings for her. I don't think twice before informing my commandant of my trip to Warsaw. There is always a chance that Zdzisiek has changed. He may not even talk to me, or worse: he will denounce me. But I sense it's not the case. And it's worth the risk. He might be going with the flow but I still trust him.

I locate Zdzisiek's one-story home in Żoliborz with no issue. During the war, I often took part in meetings in there, so when his wife opens the door, instant recognition reflects in her face. Except, now she is not as friendly as back then. She always smiled unlike now when she stares at me.

She looks both ways and wrinkles her freckled nose while running her hand through her marcel-waved brown hair. "You shouldn't be here. I saw posters of you in the city center. Please leave before you get us all in trouble."

She starts shutting the door on me but Zdzisiek's hand from behind stops her. "Honey, please make us some coffee." His voice is ordering.

She just shakes her head and moves inside, leaving us alone. "Get in before someone sees you," he urges and pulls me in. "Some of our neighbors are damn nosy." He sighs.

I bite my tongue because insulting his political choices wouldn't be a wise move right now when I need his help. "I hear you."

"Here, let's have some coffee and talk." He shrugs. "I'm sure it must be something important since you are in the open like this." His round face is serious. He still behaves in the same stern and authoritative way he did during the war.

I take the hint and ask, "You remember Anna Otenhoff?"

"Of course, who wouldn't remember such a classy woman? She returned to acting after the war, right? Witek adored her."

"Yesterday UB arrested her and brought to the Security Office in Białystok."

"What the hell. Why Białystok?"

"She was visiting my aunt," I say unable to remove a tremor from my voice. "She doesn't deserve this."

"Wait, isn't her father the war criminal who was sentenced to death, and who no one can find?"

"You know her input with the resistance."

"Of course, I do. Unfortunately, both arguments are against her and enough for UB to sentence her to death for espionage. That's the sick world we live in."

When I don't reply, staring into the table, he asks, "You care for her more than just for an old friend?"

"I do."

"What irony. I remember, when you began working for the resistance, Witek told me he thought Anna was the perfect woman for you and that you both would one day realize it."

"I can't think why he would say this." Witek never implied anything like this to me.

"He was a wise man, and for the sake of his memory, I will try get her out of this." He grins. "I suppose it's why you're here in the first place."

My breath bottles up in my chest as I make eye contact with him. "Is there anything we can do?"

He sighs. "I don't know, not until I speak to Alek Zatopolski's father who is owed some favors by President Bierut."

I don't interject, even though he is not my president. I

swallow my response and don't question any further. "I've great respect for Alek."

"I know. I do too but the only one that can help Anna is his father. I will try talking to him as soon as possible and see if he can do anything. He's our only hope." Our eyes meet. "It's a slim chance he will agree to speak for her and ask Bierut for a reprieve. So, I can't promise you much. How can I get in touch with you?"

FORTY-FIVE

ANNA

22 August 1947, UB prison in Białystok

I don't even know how long I have been in this cage-cell. There is no time in here, between the soiled cement walls, iron bed frame with flea-infested cover and window barred with wooden boards. Someone was here before me because a tin bucket in the corner is halfway filled with urine releasing fetor into the boiling air.

I'm all feverish and would give anything for a drop of water. Are they planning to starve me to death? Since they brought me here, no one has spoken to me at all. It's like they're trying to break me and get rid of me without any trouble.

At first, after my conversation with Mateusz, I was so sad that I couldn't think properly and didn't even care about being arrested. Soon though, I realized the extent of the situation and now I'm terrified. Why did they go after me here and not in Warsaw? But then everything becomes clear: someone informed them that I planned to escape abroad. Who would do that to me? I'm sure it wasn't Wanda. Maybe they have been watching me for a while and the moment I left Warsaw, they decided to arrest me.

Did they capture Mateusz too after I left him at the river? Another burst of heat runs all over my body when I think that because of me he might be in prison now. At the same time, I know he would not relent without a fight and I didn't hear any shooting on the way to his aunt's.

For the first time since marrying Helmut, I pray for strength and wisdom. I used to pray every night with Mutti but Helmut changed me and I didn't have it in me to talk to God. I even doubted his existence seeing all the terrible things throughout the war, and then after. But now I take so much comfort from the simple words Mutti taught me once.

Finally, when I'm nearly passing out, a guard unlocks the shrieking cell door and grabs my arm, lifting me up. "Get up, you are summoned for examination," he says in a loud voice.

My legs wobble and my mouth is so dry I can't swallow anymore but somehow I manage to sway my way through the putrid corridor.

The guard hurls me into the examination room and points to the wooden stool across from a desk. My vision is still blurry from being in the dark cell for so long but I don't miss a bald man in uniform who reclines in his chair and watches me with a smile. He looks so familiar.

"How's your stay so far?" he asks in deep baritone. "Did you get plenty to eat and drink?"

Unable to utter a single word from the lack of saliva, I roll my eyes. What a disgusting skunk with his dirty games.

He gives a gruff laugh revealing his yellow teeth and orders the guard to bring a cup of water and bread.

I drink the whole thing in one gulp, making myself choke, but it feels so good to have any amount of water.

The whole time his watchful eyes are on me. "You're not how I remember you. Always in beautiful dresses and stunning makeup, shining in the Café Anna. But I have to admit I like you as natural as you are now without any face paint. Your beauty is in full bloom."

My body heat rises at the sudden realization that this man is Leszek.

"I see you don't recognize me. But I was often there and always admired your beauty."

He sounds as awkward as he did back then. He thinks I don't remember him.

"Why would you pay any attention to a man like me?"

It's so hard to believe he is the same traitor that almost got us killed, and attempted to hurt me during the uprising. He looks so much older now.

"Your beautiful eyes tell me that you do remember me now. Well, we aren't here because of my infatuation with you." A smile comes and goes on his lips.

He's a watchful cad. It's as if he reads me. I brace myself to be on alert and use my best acting skills. I must guard my emotions, as the only thing I want to do right now is spit in his sleazy face. I compose a vague but guarded face expression. "What do you want from me, Leszek?"

"No worries. It's just a routine investigation we perform on many of our citizens."

I force a laugh. "I know you do." I fail to remove the sarcasm from my tone. "But why me and why on my vacation?"

"That's exactly why. When would be a better time if not now before you take a long vacation abroad?" A glimmer of laughter comes into his eyes making me flinch. "Don't worry, no one gave you away. We have just been watchful since you have refused to cooperate. If you had used your common sense and complied with our rules, your career would be at its best right now." His voice is tense. "But you're a bad girl, Anna, and we punish people such as you if they don't get their good senses back."

His aloofness makes me nervous. "I don't know what you are talking about. I only came for a brief vacation."

"Let's see if we can get some sort of collaboration here." He smirks.

The sudden shift in his attitude is relieving to me and I hope it will give me a better chance of convincing him I'm innocent and he must release me. But the moment the thought crosses my mind, I want to laugh at how naïve I am. A rat like him will stop at nothing to trap me.

"Where do I begin?" He shuffles some papers on his desk for a short moment before speaking again, "You are the only daughter of the Nazi war criminal who escaped somewhere abroad and can't be found despite his death sentence." Satisfaction gleams in his gaze. "This alone is enough for you to be accused of espionage and working against the interests of the republic the comrade Stalin is trying to build so hard for Poles."

I hold the vomit rising in my throat because I know that being rebellious will make things worse. I'm determined to survive this and stay alive. "I never agreed with my father's political views and I don't stay in contact with him."

"I do believe you. It's why you aided the Polish resistance throughout the war by fooling the German officers." He lowers his chin and looks down at me.

"These are all lies. All I did was run a café, for everyone. I needed money to survive, just like others. What's so wrong about that?" I say, not knowing what else to do. He knows very well what I did as he was a part of it, but now he's turned traitor. But I will not admit to anything he accuses me of.

He waves dismissively like my question is not worth the effort. "This alone qualifies you for one of the hardest sentences. So, if I was you, I would cooperate to keep my life." A relaxed smile crosses his face. "That's all I'm asking of you, a bit of understanding and some teamwork and you will be out, free, sooner than you think."

I have a sour taste in my mouth but I say, "What do you expect from me?"

He beams. "That's what I'm talking about." He crosses his arms. "We just need a little help from you. You see, we're having problems capturing one of the local criminals. He's very dangerous and the quicker we place him behind bars, the better for the community."

"And what do I have to do with that?" I play naïve but I know very well he is referring to Mateusz. He always hated him and obviously that hasn't changed a bit. It's comforting to know that they don't have him. A huge load lifts off my heart.

"I'm sure he still has a terrible infatuation with you, which doesn't surprise me at all. A cultured and pretty woman like you must have many admirers."

I ignore his sleazy compliment. "I don't know who you're talking about."

He smirks. "Didn't you just pay a visit to Odwaga's aunt and uncle? By the way, they are greatly respected people and we would never bother them."

"My friend gave me the address of the people I'm staying with. I only wanted to spend some time enjoying the river."

"If I didn't know any better, I would definitely believe you. That's how convincing you sound." He chuckles. "All you need to do is arrange a meeting with Odwaga through his aunt and show up. We will take care of the rest."

"I don't know the man, so this task is impossible," I say in a composed tone while fear clutches my heart.

"Enough with the games, Anna." His nostrils flare as he nears me. "If you don't agree to it, starting tomorrow we will implement more effective but also extremely painful ways to convince you. It won't be just talking; I can assure you of that." His eyes seem to bulge now.

"I don't know the man," I repeat again, thankful they didn't catch us while I was with Mateusz at the river.

"Fine." He motions to the guard. "Take her back to the isolation cell. No food and water until the next examination." Then he gazes back at me. "I hope some more time alone will make you change your mind."

"Bastard," I shout before the guard pushes me out of the room. His malicious laughter echoes through the corridor, deepening my anger.

FORTY-SIX

LESZEK

After the whore leaves, I wipe off sweat from my forehead. As I suspected, she is as stubborn as hell. If I have to, I will starve her to near-death, and then I will whip all the resistance out of her. She knows the stakes here and that I can massacre her to no recognition. And if that happens, she wouldn't be able to return to her career ever again. I'm pretty positive she will do anything to avoid such a scenario. I can't suppress the laughter that bubbles in me.

This calls for celebration. I open the lower cabinet in my desk and fish out a bottle of vodka and a glass. It's the only medication for this empty feeling inside me. It must do for now, until I have that bastard Odwaga in my hands. Then, I will finally access the true cure for all the demons that have tormented me since Celina's death.

The plan is simple. Once the German slut relents and agrees to cooperate, I will release her from the prison and she will go straight to Odwaga's aunt and express her happiness at being free again. Then, she will find a way of contacting Odwaga and setting up a meeting with him—that's when we will arrest him.

This will be his bloody end and a cheery beginning to my restoration.

FORTY-SEVEN

ANNA

Back in the cell, I collapse on the bed and stare into the darkness, determined not to shed another tear. It's time to get back to the old Anna. Considering all the dangerous games I played through the war, I can find a way with this too. It's obvious that being stubborn tomorrow and refusing to talk will bring only one outcome, one I can't even think about. I heard so many accounts of the cruel tortures and slaughter done in UB prisons. Even when it comes to pregnant women and children.

I must do everything I can to escape their cruelty, and there is only one way: I need to fool them. I will agree to their demands about Mateusz and when I'm in his aunt's home, I'll escape before even arranging the meeting. I'm sure there will be someone outside watching me the whole time but I will just have to figure this out. Maybe his aunt has a secret way I can exit the house from the back and run away. I would rather die being free than in this rat hole.

It's going to be a dangerous game, but I have no choice. Better that than staying here and letting them maltreat me. I don't know how far they would go but according to what others have said, they can be vicious. Nervous prickles run up my spine as I recall the accounts of their victims who miraculously survived. I might not have that much luck, and even if I do, I would suffer for the rest of my life from the damage they inflict.

They keep me in this suffocating cell for the rest of the day and through the night. In the morning, they bring me to the same interrogation room as yesterday. I have it all planned in my head. I will simply play my part, convincing Leszek of my cooperation, and then will see how things go from there.

"Some water?" Leszek asks as he hands me a tin cup.

I take it with my trembling hand and drink it. Then I wait for his next words, ready to agree to his terms. I will show him no rebellion, just so he believes my words.

But he stuns me by saying, "I received a very important call from Warsaw last night. Apparently, someone spoke with President Bierut on your behalf. Very well played. I have no idea how you accomplished such rare favor."

This is so unexpected that I feel dizzy. I wonder if this is good or bad news and what that really means for me. Just to be on the safe side, I remain silent.

"Our great president ordered me to set you free immediately. On one condition though." He gives me a long look like he is trying to determine my thoughts.

But I keep my face neutral and busy myself looking at my nails. This calmness is only on the outside because inside I'm experiencing an extreme adrenaline spike. "What's the condition?" I ask when he stays silent. The fact that he is so composed and that there is not a bit of anger visible in him, tells me that the condition must be too hard for me to fulfill.

"You must sign a declaration that from now on you will continue your acting career in accordance with our rules and you will be at our disposition."

My first and true instinct is to laugh in his face. Isn't that why I'm here? Because I refused that very thing. But then I remind myself that I must play along. Besides, it's a huge relief knowing that Mateusz's fate is not at stake here, only my career and good name.

I clear my throat and settle my gaze on his. I can sense he's ready for my refusal and to order torture immediately. "I agree."

His eyes widen as he scratches his jaw. "Are you certain of your decision?"

"Yes," I say, swallowing hard.

"Well, well. I see the harsh conditions have taught you a much-needed lesson." He bares his teeth. "To be honest, I didn't expect this outcome. I'm always prepared, though, and I do have the required paperwork ready for you to sign, my compeer Otenhoff."

My flesh crawls while listening to him. I never thought I would shake hands with this cad.

FORTY-EIGHT

MATEUSZ

I get into a green Opel that just pulled up on the dirt road besides the enormous alder grove. "How is she?" I ask, unable to remove panic from my tone.

Zdzisiek releases clouds of cigarette smoke and says, "Everything went according to plan. I just dropped her off at your aunt's as she wants to spend the night there and will be on the way to Warsaw first thing tomorrow morning."

I feel the anticipated release of pent-up tension. "She's going back to Warsaw?"

"That's what she said."

"I don't know how to thank you. If you ever need anything, you know where to find me."

"Thank Alek's father. You know when I told him about Anna, the first thing he did was call Alek and ask him if she was in fact his good friend." He takes another drag from his cigarette and a moment later smiles after letting out bouts of smoke. "Alek confirmed, and begged him to do anything he could to help her."

"I always knew Alek Zatopolski was one of a kind."

"Agreed. So maybe you need to thank him, instead.

Anyway, my friend, there is something else I must tell you." His relaxed demeanor instantly changes into a resigned one as he slumps his shoulders.

"What's it?" The way he said it makes me nervous. Did he compromise me? I touch my hand to the doorknob.

He notices my gesture because he says, "Relax." Our gazes meet and I see the old, dependable Zdzisiek in there. "It's about Anna."

Tremor overtakes me at the thought that she might still be in danger. "You said she is leaving for Warsaw tomorrow?"

"Yes. She signed their awful agreement, to continue her acting career under their rules, in exchange for her life." His voice fades away as my heart sinks.

"She signed," I say while conflicting emotions tug at me. It was surely the only way for her to walk out alive and untouched from this, so I'm glad she didn't refuse. But why do I feel so disappointed? I have no right to. She had to save her life and I hoped with my whole heart that she would do it. I could not go on if she didn't survive. And then, a hint of worry creeps into my mind. It means they will never leave her alone and will use her as their puppet. But most of all, she will be forbidden from leaving for abroad.

"Damn." I slam my fist into the seat. "Damn communists."

"If she didn't sign, she would be beaten and soon sentenced to death. Her fate was clear to UB, unless..." He turns his face away from me.

I take his arm. "Unless what?"

"I learned from Alek's father that when they initially arrested her, they demanded she help them set up a trap for you." He gives me a long, meaningful look. "She refused, so they accused her of espionage and partnering with her Nazi father to weaken the Polish People's Republic. Also, her collaboration with the resistance during the war dooms her even more. So, as you see, she had no choice."

"Nonsense. She doesn't want anything to do with her father." I can't stop my voice from rising. "And you mean the Stalin's People Republic?"

His face grows more serious. "Listen, my friend, I know you judged me a long time ago, and you have the right. But I will say again that the fight you're continuing is long lost and brings no good to anyone. I'm not saying this to cause you pain, and don't take it the wrong way, I'm in awe of you and the other men in there." He points in the direction of the forests. "It's just that in my opinion, there is not even the slightest chance for starting a third world war. If there was, I would be in those woods with you."

"So, you think that becoming Stalin's puppet is better for Poland?" Heat flushes through my body as I grind my teeth.

"Unfortunately, not everything in this world is black and white." His voice is quiet now and he stares into the steering wheel. "Sometimes the right choice is to blend in between, at least for the time being. I don't spread their propaganda or work in their UB prisons. I run my business helping rebuild Warsaw thanks to my plumbing abilities. It gives them the satisfaction of being able to break me and have me listed as one of them, but that's all they gained. I work for Poland and I believe with all my heart that one day we will all live in a truly independent country. But until that day comes, I want to stay alive. I know I'm losing a lot in the process—my dignity and honor as a true Pole, the name I made for myself through the war." His voice is even quieter now. "Something that is apparently most important to you. One day when we finally have our homeland back, it will be people like you that will be remembered and cherished because you represent the highest values of this nation, you give your blood in the name of your homeland. Remember my words, my friend, and know that I have the highest respect for you and others in those forests."

"But you still think that your choice makes more sense," I say, for the first time understanding his point of view.

"I do."

"You're lucky they are not forcing you into their schemes like they're going to do with Anna."

"That's true. I'm in a much better position as my occupation doesn't require as much as hers. I'm just a plumber and when it comes to the worst sacrifice it's about fixing their toilets." He smirks but doesn't smile or laugh. He knows what Anna signed herself up for. "Listen, my friend, I want to give you one piece of advice before we part. You've been a sensible man for all your life and you have a great skill to offer to this world. For God's sake, all Warsaw called you a brilliant doctor before this damned war. It's a sin to waste such talent when one day it might be one of Poland's biggest assets. Leave it all and try going abroad where you can make a life for yourself until things get better here. And trust me, they will. Not any time soon, but they will."

"It's not that easy. We've been fighting for so long believing that only one of two things can bring back independence: the war between the West and the Soviet Union or a truthful election. This is what we've been fighting for, so when one of those things happens, we are here to push it through."

"Those beliefs and that fight made sense in 1944 or 1945, but since the election in February, it's time to accept the fact that Stalin's regime won't withdraw any soon and there will be no help from the West. Churchill sold us to Stalin, and that's the truth. We are on our own."

"Corrupt and falsified election by communists, and you damn well know it."

He nods. "Listen, I know it's not easy to leave everything but the truth is that sooner or later they will slaughter you all. It's damn hard to say it, but right now there is no life here for you, and in your situation even signing their garbage papers would not prevent you from a death sentence." He puts his hand on my arm. "Take my advice and run. Poland will have its moment of freedom one day, but until it happens, we must go on with our lives."

"You know I can't do that. I believe in a different outcome than you and that there is still hope but we have to fight."

He shakes his head. "Not on an open battlefield. It's too late for that. We must fight in the way others did before us, before the 1914 war. For 123 years they held Poland in their hearts, and thanks to that we gained our independence back in 1918. You can be like Kościuszko or Mickiewicz, and many others."

That night our troops sleep in a friendly farmer's barn. I sneak out near midnight unable to sleep. I didn't agree with all of what Zdzisiek said but some things did make sense. Now I know more of his circumstances and his point of view, I would never again judge him so harshly. There are others who signed with the regime and are helping Stalin's puppets weaken our homeland. Those people are worms and just the thought of them makes me want to spit. Zdzisiek is not one of them. Definitely not, even though, I know deep in my heart I would never sign anything made by Stalin and his people. Never. My life is not worth that and never will be. There are some things that cannot be profaned. One of them is the honor of my homeland.

I can't get Anna out of my mind. Only God knows how peaceful I feel knowing her life was spared. At the same time, it pains me that she was brought between a knife and gun, and had to agree subjecting herself to something she hates with all her being. I don't view her as a traitor. I can't. Not my Anna. I did once when I thought she was collaborating with the Nazis, until I learned the truth.

My heart bleeds knowing what her life will look like. They

will never leave her alone. They will wave the paper she signed at her every time they make demands. She has no choice now but to become their puppet, unless she finds a way of leaving Poland. They would not have any power over her abroad. It's her only chance at normal life. But how far they will go, monitoring her?

I near Ciocia Krysia's cottage but stay at a safe distance. Zdzisiek said that she will be leaving first thing in the morning. Is UB watching her even now? I trail around the area trying to determine if she's being spied but I find no people lurking around nor cars shadowing nearby. It seems they left her alone for the time being.

I don't return to the barn. I stay in the garden, not far from the cottage, and when the first light shines, I hide behind the shrub near the cottage door. At this point I cease any kind of reasoning. I just need to see her, to make sure she is coping with all of this. She is like a drug to my mind and my soul and I can't go on without another look at her, another smile from her.

She slips from ciocia's home around seven o'clock, holding a small bag. Her blonde hair shines in the morning sun bringing aura of divine delicacy to her. Her beauty takes my breath away once more. I have this painful yearning in me to look in her eyes and touch her.

Without another thought I cross her path making her bump into me. I expect her to back off but she stills in my embrace. I take her both hands and kiss them while not taking my gaze off her beautiful eyes that reflect everything I love so dearly. Being able to feel her, to touch her cheek and run my hand through her soft hair puts me into the blissful state of heaven. I want nothing else from life, just to hold her like this every day for the rest of my life. And then I make a decision. I know it's the only right one. From now on, she is my priority; she is my purpose; she is my strength; she is my everything. And I feel so at peace with it. I experience the type of harmony that I never thought was possible to reach. I feel that this is the right path for me, for us, with my entire being. I hear a tiny voice inside me approving my decision, and I believe it's the voice sent to me by God.

We stay like this for a moment that seems like eternity, until she whispers, "Mateusz." Her voice breaks and she buries her face in my chest. "Please forgive me."

I tilt her chin up. "What are you saying, darling? You did no wrong."

She sobs while tears stream down her face. "I'm a traitor. I'm now one of them." She looks around. "What if they follow me." Her worried gaze keeps moving around.

"I've been watching for a while and didn't see anything suspicious. And no, you are not a traitor. I know you, you're already planning how to get out of this. Aren't you, my love?" I say and kiss every single tear off her face.

Her smile is weak, but it's there and it makes my heart beat with a strength of the hammer. "I will find a way to leave all of this behind and then they can get lost with their papers." She lifts her nose and sniffs. "I promise." A hint of arrogance gleams in her eyes.

I laugh. "I don't doubt it." I take her face in my hands. "Let's run away together where we can make a life for ourselves. Far away from here. I know that one day things will change here for good, and then we will be able to come back. We can do so much good by staying alive. We can still do so much with our lives, while keeping this homeland in our hearts."

"Are you sure?"

"Yes, I am. You mean everything to me. My life is yours. Of course, if you still want me."

"You mean everything to me too," she says deepening her gaze into mine.

"Let's find a way to go to England. I can open my practice there and you can continue your acting career." It takes all strength out of me to say this. It's not easy to leave behind everything I believe in but my love for her is stronger and I will find my way of helping this hurting homeland. I'm sure of that.

"I'd like that," she says and runs her finger down my cheek and my skin crawls with tantalizing sparks.

"I dream of nothing more right now than kissing her but I'm interrupted by a loud, menacing voice from behind us.

"Well, well, look who we have here."

FORTY-NINE

ANNA

We both jump to discover Leszek in his UB uniform, his hand holding a gun pointed at us. The bastard has been trying to chase Mateusz for so long now. How ironic that the moment we found a path for our dreams and freedom, he reached his sick goal of damning us. A hand of fear clutches at my heart, not for myself, but for my dearest Mateusz, my only treasure.

I blink away my angry tears. Why is he even here? I signed his damn papers, so what more does he want? Why does he always show up at the worst moment?

I clench my jaw and grind my teeth. "Leave us alone, Leszek," I hiss, glaring at him.

His disgusting laughter rings out, intensifying my hate. Mateusz takes my hand in his and squeezes it. He is always so quick to accept the worst fate but I'm not going to let this cad ruin everything for us.

He smirks. "I only planned to stop by this morning to ensure your swift transit to Warsaw. Never in a million years did I expect you here too, Odwaga," he lies and grins. "Looks like I will cook two bunnies in one campfire."

"Leave Anna out of this," Mateusz says, his nostrils flaring.

"I'm happy to grant your wish since she has brought you to me. The moment you are locked away, she will be free on her way to Warsaw and to her prominent career. But for now, you both are going to obediently march to my car."

"Don't you dare raise your hand at my nephew." Mateusz's aunt's stern voice comes from the back. She wears her floral apron as always, but her usually soft face now seems so sharp that for a moment I wonder if it's really her. She glares at Leszek.

"Ciocia, please go back home and stay away from this," Mateusz pleads with her. "He's not worth your time."

"Be silent, Mateusz," she barks without taking her hard gaze from Leszek.

"Odwaga is right," he says in the warning voice. "Better to stay out of this."

"Your mother must be turning in her grave seeing what you've become. Shame on you. You come from a respected family with patriotic values, and you turned into a lowlife." Through her speech, her gaze doesn't move from his. "If not for me, you would be dead a long time now, and you know it. Do you need me reminding you of the night I pulled you through that terrible infection that almost took your life away?"

The man's eyes are red now. "So what? I don't give a damn what you did, old woman. The truth is you never cared for me and my mother. Where were you when the Germans took her to Auschwitz? And why was she taken? Because she listened to you and let that Jewish woman hide in our basement. You are the one that made her do that and now she is dead." He points his gun at Pani Krysia.

"She did what she thought was right because she was a good woman, and she wanted you to be the same." Her voice is strangled now. "I could do nothing to save her."

"Of course, it's easy to wash your hands and move on with your life. In truth, you never cared that she was killed because of you." He keeps throwing his poisonous words at this poor lady who now seems so fragile as she bites her lip. Silent tears roll down her cheeks.

"Enough, Leszek," Mateusz says. "No one wants to hear your false accusations. You know my aunt cared for your mother and she proved it over and over. What happened to your mother has nothing to do with her, so enough of this nonsense."

"Then she needs to stop raving about how much she did for me and my mother. Because in the end she failed her. And you, Odwaga, always came to spend summers here and enjoyed the manor like you were privileged. You acted like you were too good for locals like myself. You always looked at us like you were a prince." His face skin stretches into a snarl. "You took my Celina away from me and you were the reason she drowned herself. That day I promised that I would find the way to make you pay for what you had done to her. I knew I would not rest while you still lived. And now the time has come."

I can't believe Leszek's ravings. How could he blame my kind caring Mateusz for all this? Especially with all they have both done in the resistance. All the suffering they have seen in the war...

FIFTY

MATEUSZ

So, this is why he's been trying to kill me? "How dare you blame me for Celina's death? I never even dated her or was close with her. You were her entire world and you failed her." I feel sorrow at the memory of Celina. I didn't know her well but I remember her as a sweet and delicate girl. Way too sensitive for Leszek who seemed always to blame everyone for his fate.

"Liar! That night when you walked together away from the campfire, you must have brainwashed her because she was never herself afterwards."

"She only needed a shoulder to cry on after you cheated on her with some other village girl. She was trying to find the strength to forgive you but she didn't trust you anymore. I only listened to her and let her cry. Whatever decision she made later, was her own." I point my finger at him. "You were the reason she took her life, so stop blaming other people."

"It's all a lie. You brainwashed her to believe I was not worth her. She would have forgiven me if not for you, damn it. You can't even imagine how much satisfaction I feel right now being the one who'll throw you into prison. Rest assured that I will enjoy each time I batter your miserable body, and then I will watch your last breath."

"I will drop dead first." Wujek Mirek stands behind Ciocia Krysia, double-barreled shotgun in his hands. At his side, Wilczur growls ready to attack. "You have done enough harm to my family." He seems so tall and powerful and the presence of Wilczur brings a hint of hope to me. But the moment the dog leaps forward, he says, "Stay." It's wise because Leszek would shoot him without hesitation.

Leszek bursts into scoffing laughter. "When was the last time you fired that ancient thing? Do you even have bullets inside it? I'm not going to fall for your pathetic attempt at saving your precious nephew."

Wujek Mirek cocks his weapon. "Try me." Wilczur bares his teeth and growls louder now. His posture betrays that he only awaits the signal from his owner to jump at Leszek.

"You damn people. I can summon the entire army here if I wish to, and you all will be done."

"Go ahead, if you stay alive that long. I don't care for my own life. I'm old, so if sacrificing myself is what it takes to end your miserable existence, I will not hesitate. Especially after all the insults you hurled at my wife, disregarding what she did for your mama and yourself. She gave her a job when your pa died and every piece of clothing you wore through your childhood came from my wife's good heart. She always cared for you like she would for her own. And look at you now ready to ruin lives of good people."

There is this hesitant look in Leszek's face but he hisses, "You're an old fool if you think I care for your pathetic words."

"I know you don't but if you care for your own life, you will walk away and never come back here. And most importantly, you will leave my family the hell alone. That's the only condition on which I will not fire this old mate of mine." He pats his weapon and grins. "Believe me, I will be happy to use it again and you will not be the first one whose life it will take away."

Leszek shrieks as his nostrils flare. "You are a mad man."

Wujek Mirek answers with a soft laughter. "Actually, when I fought in the first war, they called me the *Bloodsucker*."

Now I look at him with interest. Could it be possible that this kind uncle of mine was once a fierce warrior? I feel even more respect for him. And now he is trying to save us, probably at the cost of his own life.

"I'm going to count to five and if you don't put your gun away and walk out without ever causing trouble again, I will fire this beauty." The air becomes thick as he begins counting.

Cold sweat covers my entire body and I can't stop my face muscles from twitching. I'm ready to pounce at Leszek should I need to. But I swallow hard and something roots me into place. Every second seems like an hour and a glimpse at Ciocia Krysia's pale face and trembling chin, brings a lurch of panic into my heart.

"One, two..."

"Uncle, please don't do this," I explode. "Please take Ciocia Krysia and walk away." I hope with my whole heart that he listens to my pleading.

My uncle shakes his head. "I'm not going to be the first one walking away." It's clear that nothing will change his mind.

Leszek turns his gun in Wujek Mirek's direction and cocks it. His face is unreadable but I'm guessing he'd already made his decision. I must do everything to protect my uncle. I will jump forward, so the bullet strikes me instead. But my legs go weak.

"Three, four..." As Wujek Mirek continues counting, my body tenses and I'm about to leap forward when Leszek shouts. "Fine. Have it your way."

"*Lepiej nie wracaj tutaj, bo poszczuję cię psem.*" Better don't come back here or I will set my dog on you. Wujek Mirek's voice brims with triumph as I exhale with relief.

Leszek turns and begins walking away, just like that, but then he abruptly swirls around and fires his gun at Wujek Mirek. I release a broken sound from my lungs and leap forward. But it's too late.

Everything happens so fast, and then the next moment I know, and a few gunshots later, I stare at Wujek Mirek not believing my own eyes. He's still standing in the same position but now his weapon slides from his trembling hands.

Leszek lies motionless on the grass. I check his pulse. "He's gone."

I turn my eyes away, unable to look any longer at the terrified expression on his butchered face.

"I never thought I would have to kill this boy." Wujek Mirek's voice fades away as he covers his face in his hands.

EPILOGUE

Sixty years later

Beside me, Anna sleeps peacefully snuggled under the airplane blanket. I kiss her forehead. She's so beautiful, and that will never change in my eyes. We were blessed with incredible years together as she's been my wife since 1947. How many years is that? My mind is not the sharpest these days.

It feels impossible to grasp all these years. Mama is gone a long time now. The same with Ciocia Krysia and Wujek Mirek. Anna never heard from her father again.

And the war. I refused to remember that awful time from when it started to when I left for England. My children made efforts throughout the years to convince me to talk about it. But I just couldn't. I don't think I ever will. It's a different story with Anna. She found enough strength in her to talk about it and of her life in Germany. She's been always the stronger one of us and I pray daily that I will be the first one gone from this world.

At the age of ninety-six, I don't expect to live much longer. I've had strong faith in God for all my life, even throughout the war years. I believe we are all destined for a life beyond this one.

Anna believes in God too, even though there was a moment in her life when she refused him.

Now we are on the way to our beloved Poland. Tomorrow we will attend a ceremony with the Polish president Lech Kaczyński during which I will receive the Silver Cross of the War of Virtuti Militari with the motto of *Honor and Fatherland*. This war decoration goes back to the last king, Poniatowski, so it's one of the oldest.

There were way too many years when I doubted to see my Poland being truly free again. Even after the Gomułka's thaw in 1956, I was still among the cursed people who weren't welcome in Poland without being arrested.

The day of 4 June 1989 brought tears to our eyes: communism was overthrown. After that we visited Poland every year unless we went to visit my sister in New York, where she has built a happy life with Finn and their four children. Anna and I have three sons, eight grandchildren and five great-grandchildren. All live in London. This is the price we paid for leaving the forbidden homeland—our next generations have stronger connections to England than to our own motherland.

But dear God, how it was worth it. That day when I made the decision to leave the partisans and be with Anna, was the most meaningful day in my whole life. I chose to live, thanks to her—the only woman I've ever loved. The woman so courageous that she made me way too often feel like a coward.

Through the years, she pushed me to take on challenges, either in our personal lives or when it came to my work. She was there when I first opened my pediatric practice, but she was also there when one of my patients died. She reminded me that it wasn't my fault.

There are the two opposite qualities that define my gorgeous Anna: toughness and softness. She just knows when to ease the pressure. I thank God every day that he put her in my way. I often recall Witek's words about her being perfect for me, according to what Zdzisiek told me. How right my dear friend was.

While I focused on my practice, Anna continued her acting career, but raising our children was always our first priority. She had a successful career in the Theater Royal on Drury Lane making me so proud. Once we retired, we bought the manor house in Tosaki, the one that once belonged to my family. My aunt and uncle aren't with us anymore but I can feel their spirits in there.

Life continues to treat us well and to prove that it's important to always take the chance to live even if you have to pay a high price. In the end, it's all worth it. I'm the perfect example of that. I found my happiness, even though, at some point it seemed my fate was to die at the hands of UB.

We visit Powązki Cemetery in Warsaw during every stay in Poland and contemplate at the birch tree crosses of our friends who didn't survive the war. Witek is among them. The sacred memory of him and others will stay in our hearts until we take our last breaths.

A LETTER FROM GOSIA

Dear reader,

I want to say a huge thank you for choosing to read *The Resistance Wife*. If you did enjoy it, and want to keep up-to-date with all my latest releases, just sign up at the following link. Your email address will never be shared and you can unsubscribe at any time

www.bookouture.com/gosia-nealon

I hope you loved *The Resistance Wife* and if you did, I would be very grateful if you could write a review. I'd love to hear what you think, and it makes such a difference helping new readers to discover one of my books for the first time.

I love hearing from my readers – you can get in touch on my Facebook page, through Twitter, Goodreads or my website.

Thanks,

Gosia Nealon

www.gosianealon.com

facebook.com/GosiaNealonHistoricalFiction
twitter.com/GosiaNealon

ACKNOWLEDGMENTS

My deepest thanks belong forever to my dearest sister, Kasia, who was always unconditionally there for me throughout my life. I know with all my heart that she will truly never leave me. She is forever my beautiful sister, my best friend, my soulmate. My courageous sister never hesitated to reach for her dreams and to try new things. I followed her from Poland to New York. I never regretted my decision because I was always so close to her, my truest friend. Kocham Cię, Siostrzyczko.

I would like to thank my wonderful family for their unconditional support and love: my husband Jim; my children Jacob, Jack and baby Jordan; my parents; my nephews Matthew and Ryan, and my brother-in-law Josh; my brother Tomek; my brother Mariusz and sister-in-law Ania, my niece Ola, my nephews Gabryś and Ignaś; my parents-in-law; and the rest of my amazing family and friends whose support has been invaluable. I'm so very thankful to all of you.

Special thanks to my brilliant editor, Natalie Edwards, who is so wonderful to work with. Despite the fact that 2022 kept on bringing me down, she has been there for me with her encouragement. Thanks to her, I continue growing as an author while improving my writing skills. I know that my books benefit tremendously from her constructive feedback. She challenges me to always improve. Thank you, Natalie, for being so amazing.

Huge thanks to the entire team at Bookouture for all their awesome support.

I would like to send warmest thanks to my readers. I hope you will continue reading my books.

Gosia

Made in United States
North Haven, CT
25 February 2024

48990103R00161